Praise for *The Grunts*

Look out for:

**THE GRUNTS
IN TROUBLE**

**THE GRUNTS
ALL AT SEA**

**THE GRUNTS
IN A JAM**

Philip Ardagh

THE GRUNTS
On the Run

Illustrated by
Axel Scheffler

nosy
crow

For Scuto,
a very fine dog indeed

First published in the UK in 2015 by Nosy Crow Ltd
The Crow's Nest, 10a Lant Street
London, SE1 1QR, UK

Nosy Crow and associated logos are trademarks and/or registered
trademarks of Nosy Crow Ltd

Text © Philip Ardagh, 2015
Cover and inside illustrations © Axel Scheffler, 2015

The right of Philip Ardagh and Axel Scheffler to be identified as the author
and illustrator respectively of this work has been asserted by them in accordance
with the Copyright, Designs and Patents Act, 1988

Printed and bound in the UK by Clays Ltd, St Ives Plc

Papers used by Nosy Crow are made from wood grown
in sustainable forests.

ISBN: 978 0 85763 073 5 (HB)
ISBN: 978 0 85763 712 3 (PB)

Check out the buzz at
www.meetthegrunts.com

CONTENTS

Chapter One
Making Plans

"Sunny's right," said Mr Grunt.

"About what?" said Mrs Grunt.

"We're going to have to go on the run."

"The what?"

"The run," said Sunny. He had his hands in the pockets of his blue dress, to try to keep them warm.

"Why run?" demanded Mrs Grunt. "Why not take the caravan?"

"On the run *in* the caravan, you stuffed owl," said Mr Grunt. He was getting hot and

1

bothered and his face was red. It looked even redder against the backdrop of the snow all around them.

Mrs Grunt gave him one of her funny looks. "Then we need to hitch up Fingers," she said.

"I think we're going to have to leave Fingers behind," said Sunny. Fingers, who was technically *his* elephant, was standing right beside him. He was a very handsome elephant with very intelligent eyes, which were watching Sunny closely. The tip of his trunk was snuffling around in a large bag of stale buns with a light dusting of recent snowfall on top of them.

"Behind?" said Mr Grunt. "But he pulls the caravan!"

"I think we're going to have to leave that behind too, Dad," said Sunny.

"Behind the elephant?" asked Mrs Grunt.

"Behind. In front. Why should that matter, wife?"

"Because Fingers should *pull* the caravan, not push it, you clamshell!"

"Not if the caravan's not going anywhere, you dough ball!" said Mr Grunt.

"Shark's tooth!"

"Margarine tub!"

Mr and Mrs Grunt often talked to each other like that. Well, *shouted at* each other like that. It was their way. It doesn't mean that they didn't love each other. They did. Some husbands and wives give each other flowers. Mr and Mrs Grunt took delight in throwing insults (and the occasional melon).

"Watch-strap!"

"Foghorn!"

See?

"Here at the house," Sunny interrupted.

"We're going to have to leave Fingers and the caravan *here at the house*." The house in question was Bigg Manor (with two "g"s).

"But why?" demanded Mrs Grunt.

"Because they know about Fingers so will be on the lookout for an elephant ... and elephants are hard to disguise," said Sunny. Not that Sunny had ever tried to disguise an elephant.

This is what is called an educated guess.

And even in a jumbo-sized version of one of those all-in-one false-glasses-nose-and-moustache kits, Fingers wouldn't have looked any less elephanty.

That's the word: *elephanty*

(even if you won't find it in any dictionary unless I get there ahead of you and write it in myself).

But who was this "they" that Sunny was talking about? They were four men by the names of:

Lord Bigg (with two "g"s), bird-lover and official owner of Bigg Manor (still with two "g"s) and a parrot named Monty (with no "g"s).

Rodney Lasenby, better known as **Rodders Lasenby**, who was the former chairman of Lasenby Destructions.

Michael Jinx, a false-moustache wearer who sometimes called himself Max (brother of Mandy Jinx, who sometimes called herself Martha).

Thomas Winkle, better known as **Twinkle**,

a very large and rather frightening man in a bird suit.

Up until their escape, Bigg, Lasenby, Jinx and Twinkle had all been prisoners in Stonewell Jail.

Rodders had done some bad things in his life, such as cheating people out of their money. But the worst thing he'd done was lock his dear old mum in the cellar.

Yes: *he locked his dear old mum in a cellar*.

Not only that, he'd left her without any food or drink.

She would probably have died of hunger or thirst if she hadn't managed to tunnel her way out using her false teeth.

He shared his prison cell with the three other prisoners: the tall, beaky-nosed Lord Bigg, whose accent was even posher than

Lasenby's (which was saying something); shifty Michael Jinx, whose upper lip looked positively NAKED without a strip of fake facial hair; and a very large man indeed, who they all called Twinkle because he told them to (and he wasn't the kind of person anyone would want to argue with).

Lord Bigg was in prison for a whole variety of reasons ranging from receiving stolen goods to having an illegal firework display.

Jinx's criminal record was even MORE impressive. He was in prison for everything from reckless driving and kidnapping a man-in-a-barrel to impersonating a man with a moustache.

Twinkle was the most recent member of their cell. He'd only been there a few weeks when they planned their escape. He looked as if he should be in prison for breaking into a bank vault using just his bare hands, or illegally wrestling with zoo animals, but he had in fact been jailed for stealing eggs. Not your everyday hen's eggs you can buy in a supermarket, I hasten to add. No. He had stolen some very rare eggs belonging to a number of protected species, because Twinkle was bird *crazy*. All but one of the eggs he had stolen had been found, but the biggest and rarest of them all was still missing. Twinkle had refused to say what he had done with it.

Several years previously, Lord Bigg had sold some of the garden statues from the grounds of Bigg Manor. The man who came to take them away was Twinkle. And he had been dressed as an eagle with an orange beak and matching legs and feet. Twinkle carried the big stone statues as if they were lighter than real people. Lord Bigg watched in amazement. It

should have taken two
or three average men
to carry something of
that size and weight. And
Twinkle hadn't seemed
to tire either. He
made light work of
the second, third
and fourth statues.
His face – the only
part of him that
Lord Bigg could see
– didn't even break a sweat.

And sitting on the passenger seat of his
truck had been a dog that looked pretty much
all head, and most of that head seemed to be
made up of mouth, and most of that mouth
seemed to be made up of TEETH. The dog
– called Shark – had been very well behaved

and sat in total silence, until Lord Bigg had peered through the passenger window. Then Shark had done a very good impression of a snarling ball of hate, throwing himself at the glass and leaving lots of slobber everywhere.

Lord Bigg and Twinkle had chatted quite happily because Twinkle loved birds – the clue was in the costume, I suppose – and so did His Lordship, hence the parrot on his shoulder. The first thing Twinkle had said was, "I like your parrot, My Lord. I've got several different varieties of my own." And the conversation had gone on from there. It turned out Twinkle had an aviary – a large netted enclosure – for his birds, covering his whole back garden. He owned a lot of rare birds, some of which Lord Bigg guessed must have hatched from stolen eggs.

The next time Lord Bigg had seen Twinkle

was here in their shared cell in Stonewell Jail. It's a small world.

At first, none of the prisoners sharing that cell realised that *all four of them* had something in common (apart from being convicted criminals in the same prison sharing the same cell) until one evening, just before lights out, Rodders Lasenby had said something to Monty.

Monty wasn't a fifth cellmate. Well, in a way he *was*, I suppose. But he wasn't a human. He was Lord Bigg's parrot that I mentioned earlier and, unlike many pet parrots, he wasn't used to a life behind bars. Whereas lots of pet parrots spend most of their time in cages, Lord Bigg used to let Monty fly free. But because Monty was obviously as fond of Lord Bigg as Lord Bigg was of him – Monty particularly liked biting him – the bird chose not to fly away but to remain His Lordship's companion.

When they'd lived together at Bigg Manor, man and bird, Lord Bigg was FAR happier with Monty's company than his wife's, which was why she – Lady "La-La" Bigg – chose to live in the (very nice) pigsty with her favourite pig, Poppet. And Lord Bigg had CERTAINLY liked Monty much, much more than his five remaining servants. If any of THEM had bitten him on the nose he'd have flown into a terrible rage. But he'd let Monty the parrot get away with it on numerous occasions (which is a posh way of saying "lots of times").

And Lord Bigg had been allowed to have Monty in his cell. But only if the parrot was kept in a cage. So, in his own way, Monty was very much a prisoner too. (It also meant that Lord Bigg's face was no longer covered in lots of little sticking-plaster crosses where Monty had bitten him.)

Then came that evening just before lights out when Rodders Lasenby was passing the bird's cage on the way to his bunk and said, "Goodnight, Monty! Time for some shut-eye on my hideously lumpy mattress … and to dream of wonderful ways of getting my own back on Sunny and those dreadful Grunts."

"*G'night, Big Nose!*" squawked Monty. (He called everyone "Big Nose".)

On hearing the name "Grunt", Lord Bigg

sat up in his bottom bunk, laying aside his copy of *All About Birds Weekly*, and Michael Jinx sat up in his bottom bunk – narrowly avoiding banging his head on the bottom of Lasenby's bunk above. (Twinkle appeared to be already asleep, breathing heavily in the bunk above Bigg's, his huge hulk of a body causing a huge dip in his mattress so it looked more like a hammock. Bigg knew better than to complain. Twinkle was the sort of prisoner who you let have his own way.)

"I thought we were never going to speak of Mr and Mrs Grunt again," muttered Michael Jinx. "Or that boy of theirs in the blue dress."

"Did you say Grunts, Lasenby?" asked Lord Bigg.

"I did, Lord Bigg, I did," said Rodders Lasenby, turning away from Monty's cage. (Lord Bigg insisted his cellmates called him

Lord.) "Why do you ask? Not that I don't love being interrogated just before bed."

Just then a bell rang and Lasenby, who, like the others, was already in his regulation prison pyjamas, quickly climbed up into his top bunk. Then the lights in all the cells went out as a prison guard at the end of the corridor flicked a big red switch.

"I asked because it was the Grunts who landed me in here," whispered Lord Bigg, his words cutting through the darkness like an angry wasp with a tiny saw. "The Grunts and that ridiculous circus showman Larry Smalls."

This was, in truth, (almost) totally – well, a *bit* – untrue. Yes, Sunny and the Grunts had been there when Lord Bigg had been arrested, and yes, Mr Grunt had provided the fireworks that had meant His Lordship had had to throw himself out of a window but was later accused of setting off illegally himself … but Sunny, at least, had been trying to *save* Bigg Manor and had nothing to do with the unfortunate antics of Larry Smalls. But in Lord Bigg's enraged and mixed-up mind he had obviously convinced himself that the Grunts and Smalls were "all in it together".

"Charming people, the Grunts," said Rodders Lasenby. "Rude, unfriendly and terribly helpful. Hate 'em to bits." He was remembering being tied up in the bowels of a ship, being thrown in a police cell, being put on trial, shamed in public and ending up in jail.

"Me too," whispered Jinx, rubbing the back of his neck as *he* remembered how a well-aimed rubber tyre thrown by Mrs Grunt had knocked him and his sister Mandy off their motorbike and sidecar. "They messed up my plans and my stuff."

To be fair, what had
really landed each of them
in Stonewell Jail was their being
good-for-nothing scoundrels but, being good-
for-nothing scoundrels, they needed someone
else to blame. So they spent the next hour or so
in the darkness muttering evil thoughts about
Mr Grunt, Mrs Grunt and their son Sunny.

And when the next morning came, they
talked about the Grunts some more and they
actually hatched a plan, with Twinkle listening
with interest. Rather than simply grumbling
and going on about it, they would all four

19

– five counting Monty – escape and, rather than going into hiding or fleeing the country or starting new lives under new identities, they would track down the Grunts and GET THEIR REVENGE.

Lord Bigg liked the word "REVENGE". It has a V in it, which looks like just the kind of pointy thing he'd like to jab the Grunts in the bottom with.

Twinkle had said nothing about the Grunts during their discussions but there was no way the other three men would dare escape from their cell without asking Twinkle if he wanted to come too. He might not take too kindly to being left behind. Twinkle wasn't the sort of person anyone would want to upset. Not only that, it might be useful to take some "muscle" along with them. Secretly, Rodders Lasenby thought Mr Grunt was frightening enough, but Mr AND Mrs Grunt together? They could be real trouble.

But the prisoners had to do the escaping part first though. And escape they did.

Chapter Two.
The Visitor

The morning after the escape, Mr Grunt was having a bath. (And don't worry, I'll come back to the escape in more detail, but nobody said I had to tell this story in ORDER. Nobody said that I had to grow this beard either. I just did.) Mr Grunt usually used the old tin bath they kept in the caravan but, because the tin bath was being used for something else, he was having *this* bath in a water butt. The water butt was at the side of an old brick outbuilding in the grounds of Bigg Manor.

The house itself was in a dreadful state. For years it had looked OK from the outside but it had been pretty much stripped bare inside. Most of the floorboards had been ripped up and used as firewood. Now it didn't even look good from the outside, for reasons you'll have to read elsewhere (unless you already have).

It was a very cold morning. Mr Grunt padded across the snow in his bare feet and lifted out a perfect "O" of ice covering the surface of the water before stepping into the water butt. The water was very c-c-cold indeed. A thin layer of something oozed between his toes. At least it was the wrong time of year for the water to be filled with mosquito larvae. (Before mosquitoes become annoying whiny, bitey, airborne little insects they start off as 'orrible little wriggly water-bound thingummies, though their parents might well love them.)

"What you doing in there, husband?"
demanded Mrs Grunt.

"What am I doing? What am I *doing*?
I'm trying to get away from you," said Mr
Grunt. He was cold and his skin had gone all
goose-bumpy.

"You'll need something bigger than THAT to hide in, you pizza pan!" Mrs Grunt snorted.

"Butterbean!"

"Lung fish!"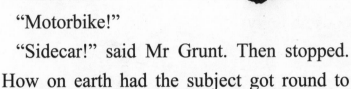

"Boot sale!"

"Motorbike!"

"Sidecar!" said Mr Grunt. Then stopped. How on earth had the subject got round to motorbikes and sidecars?

"Get dressed," said Mrs Grunt.

"Why?" demanded Mr Grunt.

"We have a visitor," said Mrs Grunt. She turned and stomped off through the snow, back in the direction of the part of the grounds of Bigg Manor where they always parked their caravan. Mr Grunt noticed that despite her wearing three cardigans AND a scarf to keep warm, she was still wearing her favourite bunny slippers rather than boots. He gave a happy sigh and began soaping himself under the armpits. (When I say "soaping", he wasn't actually using soap. He hadn't been able to find any, so was using a soap-shaped block of Cheddar cheese instead.)

On reaching the caravan, Mrs Grunt found Sunny, neck wrapped in a stripy scarf of his own, feeding Fingers. The caravan had been built by Mr Grunt and his father Old Mr Grunt, and was made from an old garden shed, part of an ice-cream van, a sidecar from a motorbike-and-sidecar – there's that phrase *again*! – and some bobs from some old bits and bobs. This extraordinary-looking vehicle had held together remarkably well.

Sunny was Mr and Mrs Grunt's adopted son. Mr Grunt had found him when Sunny was a baby, hanging from a washing line.

By his ears.

Mr Grunt had taken him home to Mrs Grunt and he instantly became one of the family.

"Where's our visitor gone?" demanded Mrs Grunt.

"I showed him into the caravan," said Sunny, handing Fingers another stale currant bun. The elephant took it delicately with the tip of his trunk and then swung it up and into his mouth. He gave Sunny a very expressive thank-you look with those highly intelligent elephant eyes of his.

"Why did you do that?" demanded Mrs Grunt.

"Because it's a cold morning, it's the polite thing to do and he has very shiny buttons on his uniform," said Sunny.

What he *didn't* say was that it was also a pleasant change to have someone in a uniform being NICE to them once in a while, rather than chasing after their caravan shouting, "I'll get you for this!" Here was someone in authority who'd been extremely polite to him and Mrs Grunt. And being polite to Mrs Grunt was not as easy as it may sound, because she was very good at rubbing people up the wrong way. She once bit a rambler who'd made the mistake of raising his cap to her and asking the quickest way into town.

"Humph," grunted Mrs Grunt. She stomped off purposefully.

Mr Grunt appeared a few minutes later. He was wearing a string vest, a shirt, a sweater (which was *almost* more holes than wool) and shoes. He had a towel wrapped round his waist, which made it look as though he was wearing a skirt. (Unlike Sunny, who was actually wearing a dress. Sunny only ever wore dresses. They were Mrs Grunt's hand-me-downs, dyed blue because he was a boy.)

"Where's this visitor then, Sunny?" demanded Mr Grunt.

"He's in the caravan having a cup of tea," said Sunny.

"Who is it?" said Mr Grunt.

"He's from Stonewell Jail," said Sunny.

"He's a prisoner?"

"No," said Sunny. "He says that his name is Mr Hindenburg and that he is the chief warder.

The person in charge."

Mr Grunt grunted and hauled himself up the steps and into the caravan, blinking to adjust to the dimmer light. He stamped the snow off his feet.

"Hello!" he called out.

"Hello!" replied Mr Hindenburg in his impressive uniform with highly polished buttons, standing up from a sofa where Mr and Mrs Grunt often sat to watch the fish swim around inside an old converted television.

He sniffed the air. He was wondering why Mr Grunt, who had so obviously just had a wash,

smelled so strongly of cheese.

Mr Hindenburg liked cheese and didn't mind cheesy smells as long as they were coming from actual cheeses. He wasn't a fan of *people* smelling cheesy.

"Who are you?" said Mr Grunt.

He told them.

Mr Grunt studied the visitor closely. "What do you want?" he demanded.

"Yes," said Mrs Grunt, pushing her way past her husband into the caravan. "What *do* you want? World peace? A slice of cake? Free slippers for life? A self-knotting handkerchief?"

"Well, I – er – I…" Maurice Hindenburg stuttered. To tell the truth, he had been rehearsing what to say when he met the Grunts but had been slightly thrown by the fact that, in no particular order:

a) the Grunts lived in such a strange caravan parked in the overgrown grounds of such a strange house
b) they had a fish tank for a television
c) Mr Grunt was wearing a towel rather than trousers, despite the freezing-cold weather
d) he smelled strongly of cheese
e) both he and Mrs Grunt seemed quite odd and very rude
f) he, Maurice Hindenburg, had bad news for them.

"I'm not sure where to begin," he sighed.

"Why not start with your socks and work up?" suggested Mrs Grunt.

"Or start with your bottom and sit down?" suggested Mr Grunt, so Mr Hindenburg did exactly that.

While Mr Grunt was talking to Chief Warder Hindenburg inside the caravan, Sunny had a visitor of his own. Unlike the prison chief warder, however, she was a regular and welcome visitor, living as she did in Bigg Manor. It was Sunny's friend, Mimi. The most noticeable thing about Mimi was how

pink she looked: pink dress, pink glasses (frames and lenses) and pink bows in her hair. She even smelled pink – if that's possible – because she'd made her own perfume from crushed pink rose petals, which is probably what attracted the two hummingbirds Frizzle and Twist, who spent much of their time flitting around above her head. Today she was wearing pink boots with a pink fake-fur trim (she would never wear REAL animal fur), a matching jacket and a fluffy pink scarf with two – you guessed it – pink pom-poms at either end.

"Hello!" said Mimi to both Sunny and Fingers, patting the elephant on his front leg, good and hard so that he could feel it through his thick skin. In return, he patted Mimi on the head with his trunk. He was very gentle.

"Mum and Dad have got a visitor," said

Sunny. "They're in the caravan."

Mimi looked surprised. "But they're not shouting."

"I know," said Sunny. "Strange, isn't it?"

"It's... It's..." Mimi tried to find the right word. "It's *extraordinary*."

They stopped and listened. They could hear the gentle murmur of voices coming from inside. Sunny stomped his feet on the snowy ground to try to keep warm.

Mimi had found a peanut and was giving it to Fingers. Fingers was a big fan of peanuts and a big fan of Mimi. He took the peanut in the tip of his trunk and then carefully popped it in his mouth.

"Are you still going out today?" asked Mimi. Sunny had a bike trip planned.

"I hope so," said Sunny. "You coming? It is a bit cold."

"If your grandpa has fixed up that bike for me," said Mimi. They went to see.

By "grandpa", Mimi meant Mr Grunt's father, Old Mr Grunt, who lived in an old shed in the grounds of the manor. He loved fixing things and making things. Sometimes he would break things just so that he could fix them. Sometimes he broke things just because he wasn't very good at making things.

They found him just outside the door, wearing no coat but three or four tatty old sweaters – making him look far, far fatter than he really was – hitting an egg cup with a hammer.

"What are you doing, Old Mr Grunt?" asked Mimi.

"Hitting an egg cup with a hammer," said Old Mr Grunt. "What does it look like I'm doing? Buttering a goldfish?"

At that moment Mrs Grunt, who'd run
from the caravan, came crashing through the
undergrowth, sending a spray of snow off
the leaves. "They've escaped!" she shouted.
"They've escaped and are coming to get us!"

"Who, Mother?" said Sunny, his heart
skipping a beat and all thoughts of a bike
ride forgotten.

"The prisoners! They've escaped and they want their REVENGE!"

Sunny had no idea what she was talking about. But *you* do, which is something.

Chapter Three

Escape!

The escape from Stonewell Jail by Lord Bigg, Rodders Lasenby, Michael Jinx, the terrifying Twinkle-in-the-bird-outfit and (not forgetting) Monty the parrot had been easy enough. The hardest part had been coming up with a way of getting out of their cell. Then Rodders Lasenby had remembered the time Monty had done the perfect impersonation of music blaring from a radio.

Many birds are good mimics. (Once, a penguin pretended to be my daughter for three years until I remembered that I didn't have a daughter, and even if I *had* had one she was unlikely to have been quite so small and to smell quite so much of fish.) Myna birds – sometimes spelled mynah birds by people who like to stick the letter "h" on the end of words*h*[1] – are particularly good at mimicking noises – everything from buzz saws to doorbells – but some parrots are pretty good at it too. And Monty really did a very good music-blaring-from-a-radio impersonation when he felt like it.

The first time Rodders Lasenby heard it he'd nearly jumped out of his prison uniform *and* his skin. Radios were banned in the cells. They were NOT PERMITTED.

Lasenby had looked around the cell to see whether it was Bigg, Jinx or Twinkle who had the illicit/naughty/not-allowed (loud) radio

[1] Sorry, that should of course be "words".

blaring out "Let Me See You Wiggle!"

When he saw that it was Monty making the racket, Lasenby laughed.

Jinx frowned. "It wouldn't be so funny if the guards heard the noise and came and turned our cells upside down trying to find a radio that wasn't there," he whined. "I hate it when they go through our stuff."

Twinkle was looking lovingly at the parrot.

"Stop worrying," snapped Bigg. As far as His Lordship was concerned, if his beloved Monty wanted to pretend to be "Let Me See You Wiggle!" playing on the radio then pretend to be "Let Me See You Wiggle!" playing on the radio he could.

Rodders Lasenby, meanwhile, was peering through the little window in the thick metal door to see if there were any guards in the corridor who might have heard Monty's excellent radio impersonation. Fortunately, there didn't appear to be any about.

And now, all these months later, Lasenby had remembered the incident. "Could you get Monty to do that 'Let Me See You Wiggle!'-playing-on-the-radio thing if you wanted to, Lord Bigg?" he asked.

Lord Bigg looked up from a jigsaw he was doing. He shrugged. "Monty does *what* he wants *when* he wants."

"I know," said Lasenby. "It really is *most* annoying. And you know how much I love being annoyed, but what I mean is, Bigg – er *Lord* Bigg," he corrected himself hurriedly. (Bigg got very annoyed if any of them ever forgot the "Lord" part.) "If you *wanted* him to make the 'Let Me See You Wiggle!'-playing-on-the-radio sound, would he do it?"

"Probably," said Lord Bigg, finding a jigsaw

piece and pushing it into place. "There are ways to encourage him."

"Why do you ask?" asked Jinx, who was busy drawing moustaches on photos of everyone he could find in a newspaper.

"Because I want the guards to think there's a radio hidden in our cell so that they search for it," said Rodders Lasenby.

"But why?" said Jinx in that whining tone of his. "You know I hate them touching my stuff."

Rodders Lasenby sighed. Jinx was very good at getting on his nerves. "Because they have to come *into* the cell to search it," said Lasenby patiently. "And to search the cell they have to unlock the door. And that gives us a window of opportunity."

"Even though that window is a door." Lord Bigg nodded. "I think you have the makings of a plan here, Lasenby! We know how to escape from the prison once we're in the exercise yard. That should be straightforward enough." It had been one of Lord Bigg's ancestors – his great-great-grandfather – who'd built the prison in the first place (though it wasn't built *as* a prison), which, as we shall see, proved to be *rather* useful when it came to escaping.

He knew family secrets that Others Did Not Know. "If we can get out of this cell, we can get out of this prison." He pushed another jigsaw piece into place. "Can you open a lock for me, Jinx?"

"You know I can't get that cell door open," said Jinx with a forlorn face. It was a dent to his criminal pride that he'd been unable to pick the lock. The only keyhole was on the other side of the door, facing the corridor.

"That wasn't the lock I was thinking of," said Lord Bigg, a big grin appearing beneath his beaky nose. "I want you to unlock Monty's cage."

Later that day – after some last-minute sewing by Jinx[2] – a prison guard named Pinkle was walking past Cell 42 when he distinctly heard the sound of "Let Me See You Wiggle!"

[2] This will be explained later. So don't get all impatient. OK?

blaring from a radio through the thick metal door. He peered through the tiny window in the top of the door.

"What's going on in there?" he demanded.

"Nothing. Nothing at all, officer," said Lord Bigg. He wasn't the best actor in the world but he was trying to sound like an even *worse* actor: doing his best to sound like someone saying, "*Nothing! Nothing!*" but meaning, "*Something! Something!*"

Rodders Lasenby, Michael Jinx and Twinkle suddenly burst into their own rendition of "Let Me See You Wiggle!" as though they were trying to drown out the sound of a radio. Twinkle's singing voice was as terrifying as he was.

"You've got a radio in there!" Officer Pinkle spluttered. "What do you think you're playing at? You know they're not allowed!" He selected one of the many keys on a long chain hanging from his belt, fingers fumbling, and put it in the lock, at the same time calling for back-up from a fellow prison guard.

Prison Officer Pinkle burst into the cell and marched over to the bunk beds from where the sound was coming. From the doorway, his back-up (Officer Gimlet) ordered the prisoners to stand facing him, against the left-hand wall. The four men did as they were told.

Pinkle, meanwhile, got down on his hands and knees and peered under the bottom bunk. What he was expecting to find was a radio. What he was met with was a parrot with a beak even beakier than Lord Bigg's nose.

Monty stopped sounding like a radio. Instead he bit Pinkle, which was why, when the prison guard stood up and turned round screaming, he had a parrot attached to his face.

And I mean *screaming*. If I were to write: *"Aaaaaaaaaaaaaaaaaaaaaaaaaaaaaaaaaaa aaaaaaaaaaaaaaaaaaaaaaaaaaaaaaaaaaaa aaaaaaaaaaaaaaaaaaaaaaaaaaaaaaaaaaaa aaaaaaaaaaaaaaaaaaaaaaaaaaaaaaaaaaaa aaaaaaaaaaaaaaaaaaaaaaaaaaaaaagh!"* *said Prison Officer Pinkle*, that wouldn't do justice to the noise he actually made.

Without a moment's hesitation, Officer

Gimlet dashed across the cell to help his fellow guard. Before you (or anyone) could say, *"You shouldn't have left the doorway unguarded!"*, Lasenby, Jinx, Bigg and Twinkle were sprinting for the exit. As Gimlet passed him, Jinx cut the prison guard's key chain with a pair of bright-pink-handled wire cutters his Auntie Bid had sent him in a cake tin. (The guards had been so busy searching the cake for tools and weapons baked inside it that they'd completely overlooked the tin it came in, which had a false bottom.) Jinx grabbed the keys.

Reaching the doorway, Lord Bigg paused long enough to say, "Come on, Monty!" and before the two prison guards had time to work out what was happening, the parrot unattached himself from Pinkle's head, flew across to the doorway and landed on Bigg's shoulder. With

the four prisoners out in the corridor, Jinx swung the thick metal door to their cell shut and locked it with one of the stolen keys.

"Awfully well done, chaps, and all that," said Rodders Lasenby. "That went remarkably smoothly and I do like smooth things except, perhaps, for peanut butter. I much prefer crunchy peanut butter." (I don't like peanut butter at all, in case you were wondering.)

They ran down the corridor, through an outer door – opened by another of Officer Gimlet's keys – and into the exercise yard. Freedom was so close they could almost taste it.

It took a while for Sunny to make sense of what Mrs Grunt was saying as she ran around outside Old Mr Grunt's shed, twice tripping over and ending up in the snow.

"What escaped prisoners, Mum?" he asked.

He guessed she must have got the prisoners part right because the chief warder of Stonewell Jail was sitting in their caravan and he was unlikely to have popped by just for a friendly chat. Mrs Grunt didn't really do friendly chats.

"And who do they want their revenge on?" Mimi asked, Frizzle and Twist dancing around above her head.

"Some escaped prisoners want revenge on us because we upset them, according to *him*." Mrs Grunt snorted. "Us, upset people? Seems unlikely to me."

Considering there were few things in life Mr and Mrs Grunt enjoyed more than stopping and pointing and laughing at people it seemed VERY likely that they upset at least one person most days.

Chief Warder Hindenburg appeared through

the undergrowth, being careful not to get his splendid uniform (with the shiny buttons)

too wet with snow. He went up to Sunny and shook him by the hand. Having met him and his adoptive parents, Maurice Hindenburg (quite rightly) realised that, despite his blue dress, sticky-up hair and wonky ears, Sunny was obviously the most sensible one around there. Catching sight of a bearded old man with a very large hammer talking to a VERY pink girl with a couple of hummingbirds humming above her head, he wasn't about to change his opinion. "Thank you for the tea," he said.

"My pleasure," said Sunny.

Mr Hindenburg wouldn't have said that if he'd been served the usual Grunt brew. They had two types: tea made from a teabag reused so many times that you might just as well have poured water on to a sock; and "tea" made from anything that looked vaguely like tea leaves, which could be anything from ashes to badger dandruff.

Luckily for Mr Hindenburg, though, a few weeks previously the Grunts had been visited by their old friend Speedy McGinty, the well-known wheelchair athlete. When Speedy visited, she brought real coffee and real tea.

The chief warder of Stonewell Jail held out a piece of paper. "Here are the names of the four escaped prisoners," he said.

Sunny took it and glanced down at the names on the list. He recognised three of them at once. Suddenly everything made a sort of sense.

"And we found this hidden in their cell behind a loose brick in the wall under the bunk bed," said Hindenburg, handing him a second piece of paper.

It had been scrunched up but then smoothed flat. On it, three names appeared again and again: MR GRUNT, MRS GRUNT and SUNNY, and there were lots of rude words and crossings-out and pictures that were obviously supposed to be of MR GRUNT, MRS GRUNT and SUNNY with terrible things happening to them, such as being attacked by geese and being flattened by a giant boxing glove attached to a wrecking ball on a crane. Even the three of them being stuffed head-first into a beehive!!! Right across the middle of the paper, in red jagged letters, was the word "REVENGE".

"It seems that at least one of them has got it in for your family," said the chief warder, "and when we checked the files we found that you were involved in three of the four arrests."

"Wow," said Sunny. "This is serious."

"Yes," said the man. "Good luck, Sunny. Look after yourselves. And stay alert." He raised his cap with the impressive gold badge in the middle.

"Yes. Right. Thank you," said Sunny. "Will do."

Maurice Hindenburg turned and disappeared through the undergrowth, back the way he'd come. He'd done his duty and now wanted to put plenty of distance between himself and the crumbling manor with its wild gardens, the extraordinary caravan and, of course, the Grunts themselves.

57

The previous day, having just escaped from Cell 42 with a little help from a talented parrot, the four prisoners were now dashing into the exercise yard. One of the prisoners' jobs was to shovel snow, so the yard was snow-free and the flagstones gritted. The rest of the prisoners were now in lock-up – locked in their cells – so the yard was empty. The four men hurried over to the middle where there was a big old circular stone well, from which Stonewell Jail got its name.

Over the years a number of prisoners had tried escaping by diving into the well to see if it led to a big pipe or some underground cavern. In fact, the well was fed by an underground spring coming from a very narrow gap in the rock, so the prisoners had to give up and return spluttering to the surface. The ones who hadn't drowned, that is.

The names of the prisoners who *had* drowned were written on a plaque screwed to the side of the well. At the top of the plaque it read:

THE FOLLOWING PRISONERS WERE DUMB ENOUGH TO TRY TO ESCAPE DOWN THIS WELL AND DUMB ENOUGH TO DROWN

which wasn't very nice (but I suppose it was designed to stop other poor unfortunate prisoners trying it and ending up dead). Nowadays there was also a large metal grille padlocked in place over the top.

But those prisoners didn't know what Lord Bigg knew. Many, many years before, his great-great-grandfather had been stinking rich, ridiculously rich, rich BEYOND rich and had had a castle built, just for the fun of it. And because he wanted it to be FUN, he hadn't had it built like a real castle but like a castle in an adventure story, full of secret passages and hidey-holes and turrets and endless twisting staircases. However, when the Bigg family finally lost their family fortune, the castle was sold along with just about everything else except for Bigg Manor. And the castle was turned into Stonewell Jail.

Now, it's not a good idea for a prison to have lots of secret passages for prisoners to escape down, or hidey-holes to hide in, so the prison authorities had gone to a great deal of trouble to rip out and change the inside of the building – because it was still far cheaper than having to build a prison from nothing, and because it had satisfyingly thick stone walls. They were provided with a set of original plans that showed where the hidey-holes and secret passages were, which made their job so much easier.

But there was one secret passage that didn't appear on the plan, the whereabouts of which was passed down from generation to generation of Biggs. Why? For fun? Because knowledge is power? Just in case? Who knows ... but the information was about to come in very handy.

Pulling a hairpin from the top of his sock – the same hairpin he'd used to unlock Monty's cage – Jinx picked the padlock that was holding the grille over the top of the well. He flipped back the grille and peered at the surface of the water about two metres below.

"What now?" demanded Twinkle, his breath spiralling up into the cold air above his huge padded eagle's beak, like steam.[3]

"Follow me!" said Lord Bigg. He sat on the stone rim of the well and swung himself round so his feet were now in the well.

[3] In fact, the stuff you see coming out of a boiling kettle's spout is water vapour. The gap between the end of the spout and the start of the vapour is the actual steam (invisible to the eye). So there.

Monty hopped off His Lordship's shoulder and paced up and down the side of the well in birdy strides. Carefully, so very carefully, Lord Bigg lowered himself into the well, still holding on tight to the rim. He scanned the stonework walls, looking for something.

At that moment a siren sounded. Their escape was being announced to the whole prison.

"Now might be a good time to hurry, old bean," said Rodders Lasenby, peering down at Bigg. "Not that I mind my heart beating this fast. It makes me feel alive!"

Lord Bigg gave Lasenby the benefit of a withering look and brushed aside a fern growing out of the curved well wall with the toe of his prison-issue boot. It revealed a stone shaped like an egg. He gave it a sharp KICK. (Mr Grunt would have loved that part. He did so enjoy a good kick. He'd recently kicked a display of neatly stacked cans of beans in Hall's Groceries. What had made it all the more satisfying was that most of the falling cans had landed on Mrs Grunt.)

Lord Bigg gave the stone a second kick. There was a GRAUNCHING sound and, for the first time in nearly one hundred and sixty-five years, a much larger section of stone slid away to reveal an opening. Before you could say "Be careful!" Bigg had swung himself feet-first into the opening and let go of the rim of the well. He disappeared into the secret tunnel (which was more of a slide down a chute).

Without a moment to lose, Rodders Lasenby had swung himself into position and followed with surprising agility. Next came Twinkle. It wasn't that easy for him. He fitted into the opening of the well all right – though it wasn't necessarily a comfortable fit – but the secret tunnel/chute was a different matter. It was a bit like a tight-fitting cork (dressed as an eagle) trying to work its way into the neck of a bottle.

After what seemed an age to Jinx, who was waiting to go next, Twinkle's head finally disappeared from view. Jinx had managed to lift the metal grille back over the top of the well with one hand – causing Monty to take flight – as he lowered himself in the opening. The grille fell into place above him. He reached through and clicked the padlock shut again behind them.

Moments later, a gaggle of panicking guards spilled out into the exercise yard, blowing whistles, waving batons and even wielding torches.

"Look!" cried Prison Officer Gimlet, pointing up at Monty, who was flying up and over the prison walls.

On seeing the prison guards, Monty changed his gleeful parroty squawks of "*Hello, Big Nose! Hello, Big Nose!*" to a different sound: that of "Let Me See You Wiggle!" playing on the radio.

Chapter Four

Pig Bus!

In the days before Fingers the elephant pulled the Grunts' caravan, that job had belonged to a pair of donkeys, Clip and her brother Clop. The only way you could easily tell the donkeys apart from a distance was by their ears. They looked like the hands of a clock and each donkey's ears appeared to be showing a different time. The Grunts' caravan was an enormous great thing and the donkeys weren't getting any younger. In fact – because time is always moving in a forward direction (unlike the hands of their ear-clocks) – they were getting older.

"But they're still young enough to be able to carry me," Mrs Grunt insisted. She was clutching a few of her most treasured possessions, including a chocolate-coloured cat-shaped doorstop she called Chocolate Biscuit and a stuffed hedgehog she'd named Sharpie.

"They'd only slow us down, Mum," said Sunny.

"And you on a donkey would be as unusual and as easy to spot as Fingers, Mrs Grunt," said Mimi.

Mrs Grunt gave her *another* one of her funny looks (which describes just about any of her looks because she was funny-looking).

"I still don't understand why you don't ask for police protection," said Mimi. "If they know that there are some escaped prisoners out to get you, surely they can put you somewhere safe?"

"We've talked about this, Mimi," said Mr Grunt. "I've never had a very good time with the police—"

"We had a good time with Police Constable Barks," Mrs Grunt reminded him. "Singing and dancing and drinking nice drinks."

"The only reason we had a good time with PC Barks was because he was handcuffed to me at our wedding, you brass hinge!" said Mr Grunt. "Of course we had a good time. I was marrying *you*…"

There was a stunned silence. It lasted long enough for Sunny to count silently: *One-hippopotamus, two-hippopotamus, three-hippopotamus, four-hippo—*

Mr Grunt had accidentally said something NICE about Mrs Grunt during an argument.

"Well, he must have been a very naughty policeman for being handcuffed in the first place," said Mrs Grunt, having regained her composure.

"I was handcuffed *to him*, remember?" said Mr Grunt. "It was that business about the missing ice-cream van. What would I want with an old ice-cream van?"

"Too right." Mrs Grunt nodded.

Sunny looked over to their caravan, part of which still had the faded pictures of two ice-cream cones and an ice-lolly on the peeling paintwork.

"Turned out Calico Joe had eaten the van for the insurance, remember?" said Mr Grunt.

Sunny felt a flutter of relief in his chest. He didn't like to think that the home he'd always known and loved was made of "borrowed-without-asking" parts.

"There are probably quite a few policemen and women in quite a few counties who'd like to have a word with Mum and Dad about quite a few…" Sunny paused to find the right word, "…*misunderstandings*," he told Mimi.

Mimi nodded. "I should have thought of

that," she said. "Of course you can't ask for police protection!"

"I don't want to see them behind bars again," Sunny whispered, which gives me an excuse to reuse this illustration of Mr and Mrs Grunt. (The bandage was the result of a squirrel bite.)

Sunny ran his fingers through his sticky-up hair, an action that didn't make it any less sticky-up but did help him think. "Mum. Dad. We must leave the donkeys here. Peach is going to give us a lift to the station. We'll get the train to Hutton's Vale Halt, then go to Speedy's bungalow where we can lie low for a while."

"Do we have to lie *low* because it's a bunga*low*?" asked Mrs Grunt.

"No, we have to lie *low* because you're an idiot," said Mr Grunt.

"It takes one to know one," said Mrs Grunt.

"Are you calling me an idiot?"

"Well, I'm not calling you a minicab."

"So you're all going to hide out at Speedy's home and hope that the police capture the escaped men in the meantime?" said Mimi.

Sunny could tell she was worried, even with her eyes mainly hidden by her pink-framed, pink-tinted glasses. "Yup."

"And you're absolutely sure you don't want me to come with you?" said Mimi.

"It's important that you stay here to look after Fingers and the donkeys," said Sunny. He made no mention of Old Mr Grunt, who'd stubbornly refused to come with them.

"I'll do my best," said Mimi.

"We'll only be at Speedy McGinty's until the heat's off," said Mr Grunt.

"Who put the heat on in the first place?" demanded Mrs Grunt. Because it was winter she was wearing three cardigans, only one of which was back to front. On her head she wore an elf's hat. Of course, there are no such things as elves – in this country at least – but she'd found it in a box of

74

old abandoned Christmas things round the back of a church hall somewhere, and thought it rather suited her. (It didn't.) "I don't think it's hot," she said.

Sunny sighed. "When did Peach say he'd get here, Mimi?"

"Soon," she said.

"I do hope so," said Sunny. "I really do."

It was quite a hair-raising ride down the secret chute from the stone well at Stonewell Jail, not that Lord Bigg and Rodders Lasenby had much hair between them and it was hard to know how little or much hair Twinkle had under that bird outfit of his. Michael Jinx was hairy enough on the top of his head and all over his body but, truth be told, he felt naked without his false moustache. (When Lasenby had asked him why he didn't simply grow a real one, he'd whined, "But then how could I disguise myself?")

Having been first in the chute, Bigg was first out, landing with an "OOF!" on what must have once been some thick padding designed to cushion the abrupt arrival. Being so old, however, it'd long since turned to rags.

He had the sense to roll quickly out of the way, making room for Lasenby's arrival.

"Oof!" went Lasenby.

"Get out of the way, man!" Bigg warned.

"Yes… Quite!" said Lasenby, rolling the opposite way to Bigg.

He needn't have rushed. Rather than slide down the chute at speed, Twinkle became wedged more than once and had to elbow his way down the tighter parts.

He slowly emerged, (eagle-)feet-first, at the bottom and pulled himself out and upright.

Then Jinx's feet appeared at the end of the chute, swiftly followed by the rest of him.

The four men dusted themselves down.

Jinx looked into the gloom. They were in a small room built of the same stone as the prison. A wide passageway stretched ahead of them into darkness. "You say this will lead us to the grotto?" he asked. He sounded doubtful.

"Yes," said Lord Bigg, "if the family secret is accurate, which it has been so far."

"It had better be," said Twinkle matter-of-factly, the suggestion being that if the passage *didn't* lead them to the grotto someone might get their bones broken and it wouldn't be him.

Lord Bigg had told his cellmates all about where – according to his father, the previous Lord Bigg – the other end of the secret passage was supposed to come out: in the shell grotto in Meandering Gardens. Meandering Gardens had been the grounds of yet another Bigg family property but the house itself had long since gone. The grounds were now a public park and were beautifully looked after, along with the remaining outbuildings, including the shell grotto...

After a fifteen-minute walk, Lord Bigg, Rodders Lasenby, Michael Jinx and Twinkle arrived at a blank stone wall.

"Now, we'll either find that the exit was blocked up years ago and that we're trapped in here and could die here," said Rodders Lasenby, "which is probably slightly less exciting and romantic than it sounds. Or we could be—"

"Just moments from freedom," said Lord Bigg. He pressed a stone, similar in shape to the egg-shaped stone that he'd kicked in the side of the well.

Nothing happened.

He pressed again.

"Let me try," said Jinx. He jabbed the stone with his finger a few times.

Still nothing.

Hulking-great Twinkle lumbered forward and gave the wall a kick Mr Grunt would have been proud of. He was instantly rewarded with another GRAUNCHING sound. The wall became a door, sliding open and then jamming, but still having opened wide enough for each of them – even the hulking-great Twinkle in his eagle outfit – to *squeeeeeeeeeze* through the gap.

They found themselves in a human-made cave with walls covered in glittery mosaics that were studded with real shells. This was indeed the grotto. In the corner, on a stone bench, sat a park keeper dressed in a bright-red lobster suit with a sign round his neck that read "WINTER WONDERLAND". He was snoring gently and missing all the excitement. Twinkle, Lasenby, Jinx and Bigg walked out through the entrance.

They were free.

Yes, Sunny had been expecting Peach to arrive. Yes, Sunny had been expecting Peach to be driving. But no, Sunny *hadn't* been expecting Peach to be driving the Pig Bus. When the two had first met, Peach was still Lord Bigg's butler. He'd hated His Lordship and he'd hated the job. When Lady "La-La" Bigg had managed to free him from his contract (and anyway, Lord Bigg had been put behind bars), he'd become the manager of her local inn, The Happy Pig.

La-La Bigg loved pigs because they reminded her of the snorting noises made by her son Horace (who'd been missing for *years* but was now found). She even lived in a pigsty with her best friend Poppet.

Her most recent purchase for The Happy Pig was the Pig Bus, for driving customers to and from it. If you were a pig fan, it was a wonder to behold. It was a bright-pink pig-shaped minibus, with a head at the front and a curly tail at the back, and windows at the side. Not only that, it made a grunting noise as it was driven.

"You're going in *that*?" Mimi gasped. "I thought you wanted to blend into the background. Wasn't that the whole point of leaving Fingers behind?"

Peach pulled the Pig Bus to a halt, sending a spray of slushy snow over the kerb, and switched off the engine. The grunting stopped.

"This is only a trip to the station," said Sunny, thinking fast. "People will be so busy looking at the Pig Bus itself, they probably won't give us passengers a second glance. It's like hiding in the wide open. This could be *good* for us."

Mimi looked doubtful. She'd need more convincing. "I wish I was coming with you," she said.

"There's no one else I could trust to look after Fingers and Clip and Clop," said Sunny. "And, more to the point, Fingers trusts you. You couldn't be helping us more."

Mimi went pink with pride, which made her match her pink glasses frames, tinted pink lenses, pink bows, clothes and shoes even MORE. The hummingbirds, Frizzle and Twist, flitted above her head.

(Want to know a secret? Mimi was never

a big fan of pink. Not only that, she found the idea that any colour should be "a boy's colour" or "a girl's colour" faintly ridiculous. The reason she wore pink dated back to when she'd worked for Lord Bigg as a bootboy, and she was a girl. But Lord Bigg had said that there was no such job title as bootgirl so she had to remain a bootboy. So she'd decided to try to look and smell like the most girly bootboy there'd ever been. And now that she was a do-whatever-you-feel-like tenant living rent-free, she'd stuck with the look because she and everyone around her were used to it. But pink? Personally, she could take it or leave it.)

Peach had appeared in front of them. "All set, Sunny?"

"If you could help me persuade Mum and Dad to travel light, then I think so," said Sunny.

Mr Grunt had managed to get together one large, folded, itchy blanket and eleven non-matching cases, and had filled them with rocks. (Just the suitcases, not the blanket.) This was just to make sure there were no suitcases left for Mrs Grunt and that they'd be too heavy for her to lift.

In the end, Sunny, Mimi and Peach between them managed to convince him that it was better not to take any of them. Just the blanket.

When it came to Mrs Grunt, she had a small string bag containing clean underwear, Chocolate Biscuit, Sharpie and a few melons (in case of accidents). The Grunts had discovered that a cooling melon-half could help soothe most lumps, bumps, scrapes and breaks.

Old Mr Grunt had refused all efforts to go into hiding with them, so Mr Grunt had tried rolling him up in a carpet to force him to come but had failed.

"Silly old codger," muttered Mr Grunt, but it was obvious that he was worried.

"You could check up on him once in a while, Mimi," said Mrs Grunt. "But the donkeys come first, then the elephant and *then* Old Mr Grunt."

"I will!" said Mimi.

"All aboard!" said Peach, stepping back into the driver's seat.

Mr and Mrs Grunt and Sunny clambered aboard the Pig Bus, Mrs Grunt's bunny slippers wet through with snow. The engine started and so did the grunting, and they were off.

When Lady "La-La" Bigg had first bought the Pig Bus it had caused a lot of excitement in the local press. One local headline read:

LA-LA HAS A BRAND NEW PIG BUS

which Lady Bigg thought sounded rather good but was slightly bothered that it might suggest she had an *old* Pig Bus that she was replacing, which wasn't the case.

When it first took to the streets, everyone stopped and cheered or laughed and waved. (The Grunts laughed and pointed and once, when the Pig Bus had stopped at a set of traffic lights, Mr Grunt had even been able to give one of the back wheels a most satisfying kick.) Now locals were far more used to it but it was impossible to get *totally* used to a Pig Bus, especially when you didn't know when or where it might appear.

Mr and Mrs Grunt and Sunny were the only passengers on board for this special trip to the station. They could sit anywhere, which was another way of saying that Mr Grunt wanted to sit wherever Mrs Grunt wanted to sit and Mrs Grunt wanted to sit wherever Mr Grunt wanted to sit, which is why the pair of them ended up standing most of the way.

Sunny sat at the back with the bulging string

bag and a folded large, itchy blanket on his lap.

When they arrived at the station, ready to catch the train to Hutton's Vale Halt, Mr Grunt unfolded the large, itchy blanket and insisted that all three of them get under it. "That way no one will recognise us."

Sunny wasn't quite so sure but thought it better to get it over and done with rather than stop and argue about it, which might attract even more attention. They somehow managed to get themselves and their luggage aboard without incident. Once on the train Mr Grunt got his foot tangled up with the blanket and fell over, causing the others to fall on top of him. They became wedged in the corridor of the train.

Each railway carriage was divided into compartments – separate little "rooms" –

and there were two ways to get into each compartment. There was a door on one side that led directly in and out of the compartment. Passengers could only use these when there was a platform on that side of the train, of course. When people were stepping aboard the train from a platform on the *other* side – or were already on board but wanted to change compartments – there was a long corridor, with an indoor sliding door into each compartment.

Why am I telling you all this? Because Bigg Station only had one track passing through it. This meant people could climb aboard the train from either platform on either side …

… and while Mr Grunt, Mrs Grunt and Sunny were writhing around in a tangled blankety heap in the corridor, a small group of people – including one in a bird suit and another with a parrot – were slipping through a door into the next-door compartment, *in the same carriage*, from the other side.

Chapter Five
Trouble Brewing

The first thing Lord Bigg, Rodders Lasenby and Michael Jinx did when they left the shell grotto in Meandering Gardens was go behind a big snow-covered bush and turn their prison jackets inside out. This wasn't as crazy as it sounds. Jinx was rather good at sewing, so had added various pockets and lapels to the insides of their jackets in advance of their escape.[4]

Now they wore the inside on the outside, their prison jackets looked far less like

---

[4] See. I TOLD you you'd find out what the sewing was all about back on page 45. Would I lie to you?

prison jackets.

"I look like a banker down on his luck," said Rodders Lasenby, "which is a very good look to have." He looked Jinx up and down. "You look like some kind of weirdo," he announced. "Excellent disguise."

Jinx muttered something under his breath.

"And me?" asked Lord Bigg, raising an eyebrow and removing a seemingly invisible piece of lint from one of his sleeves.

"You look like a gentleman, Your Lordship," said Lasenby. "I'm afraid there's nothing we can do about that."

The fourth member of the escape party simply stood there in his bird outfit watching the other three. He said nothing. Now, it may have occurred to you that no matter how well disguised the other three were, if Twinkle stayed in his bird outfit it would be pretty obvious to anyone on the lookout for them that they were the escaped prisoners.

I'm sure that it had occurred to all three of *them* too. But which one of them was going to be brave enough and/or stupid enough to tell a man the size of a portable mountain that he needed to change into something different? They valued their heads remaining attached to their bodies by way of their necks. So they said nothing and all three of them shivered, partly through fear and partly because it was so, so cold.

"We really should get moving, chaps," said Rodders Lasenby. "Soon there will be police looking for us everywhere. Which will be very exciting, of course, but—"

"I know of a place where we can hide out for the night and make plans," said Lord Bigg. "Not far from my old home and from those *Grunts*." He made the name sound like a very nasty word indeed.

The "place they could hide out for the night" was a HUGE garage. (It was more like a small aircraft hangar.) As well as houses, islands, works of art and mechanical animals, some of Bigg's ancestors had also collected vintage cars. These had all long since been sold, but a huge garage in which some of the cars had been stored still remained. It wasn't in the grounds of Bigg Manor but several miles away, up a short driveway at the edge of an overgrown field.

When they reached it, Jinx's face dropped. "It's bad enough we're going to be sleeping in a garage, but this … this is a dump!" His voice was as whiny as a mosquito trapped in a jar.[5]

[5] Which means that it was VERY whiny indeed.

Dump might have been a bit of an exaggeration, but it was certainly two other words beginning with d: derelict and dilapidated, which meant that it was a *bit* of a dump (which begins with b). The roof – currently covered in a thick layer of snow, of course – had sagged and collapsed in a number of places, leaving gaping holes. A tree had grown up through the concrete floor in one corner and there was a lot of dead mile a minute (also known as Russian vine by people who want to make it clear they're talking about a plant). But the walls were mainly solid and only one of the two huge doors at the front was hanging off its hinges.

"I think it has a certain rustic charm," said Rodders Lasenby as he strode in and looked around. He eyed the tree and dead vine. "See? It even has built-in houseplants!"

"We'll freeze," said Jinx. "I wish I could have brought my stuff with me."

"Nonsense," said Twinkle.

No one was about to argue with him. Rodders Lasenby was sick to the back teeth of Jinx going on about his "stuff" anyway.

"This is more indoors than outdoors and there's plenty of sacking over there for us to use as bedding," said Bigg. His Lordship pointed to a large pile of brown hessian sacks against a wall. They were stamped "BIGG RAILING COMPANY".

"And we could make a fire in here," said Lasenby, rubbing his hands together enthusiastically. "No need for a chimney with all these holes in the roof."

"No," said Lord Bigg.

"No?"

"No. Because the police will be out looking for us by now and smoke pouring out of an abandoned building is bound to attract attention."

"How utterly annoying," said Rodders Lasenby, "and a very good point, Your Lordship."

Come nightfall, each man sat on a sack to try to protect themselves from the chill of the concrete floor, and were wrapped in as many of the other sacks as possible. They looked a sad sight huddled together – three men and a giant sort-of-bird – as they made their plans.

But they were talking fighting-talk.

If all the elements of their plan came together it was a straightforward one: Rodders Lasenby would use his old business contacts to have a GREAT BIG CRATE delivered to a prearranged spot. They would then capture the Grunts, put them in the crate and have it collected and shipped to the middle of nowhere. Simple. If all the in-between bits worked out.

And although "if" is about as small a word as you can get (apart from "a" and "I"), this particular "if" was a BIG "if".

"I may no longer own my company," said Rodders Lasenby, referring to Lasenby Destructions, "but there are still people working there who owe me favours. They can deliver us a crate *and* later have it shipped to the middle of nowhere."

"Where exactly is the middle of nowhere?" asked Jinx. "I've been meaning to ask."

Twinkle glared at him. "You know nowhere?" he said slowly.

Jinx decided that it was best to say yes and get the conversation over as quickly as possible.

"Well. We're going to send them right into the middle of it."

"Right," said Jinx.

"Utterly ridiculous!" said Lasenby. "And I do *so* like an utterly ridiculous idea. Perfect."

Lord Bigg raised an eyebrow. "Tomorrow

we have to get you to a telephone so that you can arrange that crate, Lasenby," he said. "In the meantime, we need to try to get some sleep."

🔑

Mr and Mrs Grunt fought to see who could get into their carriage first. As so often happened when a doorway was involved, they became wedged in it, blocking the train corridor at the same time.

"Move, you throat gargle!" snapped Mr Grunt.

"No, *you* move, you jellied eel!" said Mrs Grunt.

"Softball!"

"Fairy cake!"

"Handstand!"

"Goat's cheese!"

"Goat's cheese?" spluttered Mr Grunt. "Did

you just call me goat's cheese?"

"No," said Mrs Grunt indignantly, still trying to push herself free and into the empty compartment.

"Did!"

"Didn't!"

"Did!"

"Didn't," said Mrs Grunt.

"*Diiiiiiiiiiiiiiiiiiiiiiiiiiiiiiiiiiiiiiiiiiiiiiid!*" cried Mr Grunt, breaking free and tumbling to the floor.

"Ha!" said Mrs Grunt, stepping over him and sitting herself by the window.

Mr Grunt glared at her bunny slippers. The bunny slippers seemed to glare back at him.

Sunny entered the compartment as Mr Grunt struggled back to his feet. The boy was now carrying the large scratchy blanket and the string bag containing Chocolate Biscuit (the cat-shaped doorstop).

Now that Lord Bigg, Rodders Lasenby, Michael Jinx and Thomas "Twinkle" Winkle had escaped from prison and had had a relatively-all-right night's sleep, Jinx thought that it was time to help his sister, Mandy, escape from *her* prison.

"That wasn't part of the plan," said Lasenby.

"We never had a proper plan," Jinx pointed out. "But now that we're free, it's only fair that we try to free Mandy too. She has as much reason to hate the Grunts as the rest of us. And anyway, she and I always work as a team."

"But that could take days. Months, even," said Rodders Lasenby. "We were lucky. We had a secret escape tunnel all ready and waiting."

"It'll take next to no time," said Jinx. "She's in an open prison."

"No roof?" asked Twinkle.

Jinx explained that what he meant was that Mandy wasn't in a high-security prison. It was one of those prisons where, except for when they were locked in at night, the prisoners – all women (it being Langley Women's Prison) – were trusted to behave themselves. In fact, one year more than three hundred women absconded – which is prison-speak for escaped

– which is odd because there were only two hundred and eighty prisoners at the time.

Following this mass breakout, a new chief warder was put in charge and she asked even *more* nicely for the prisoners to behave and to be in their cells and ready to be locked in by 8 p.m. and for lights out at 9 p.m. This time, three hundred and sixty women escaped from the prison. The additional sixty prisoners had come over from a nearby open prison to join in the mass escape for the fun of it.

Since then new rules had been put in place and the odd prisoner had escaped – and some of them really were odd – but very few.

"We can't go, I'm afraid, Jinx," said Bigg. "We really—"

"We're going," Twinkle announced. The tone of his voice didn't leave any room for argument.

"It's not fair to leave his sister behind."

"Um … very well," said Lord Bigg. "Then we shall go at once!"

When Bigg, Lasenby, Jinx and Twinkle arrived at Langley Women's Prison they couldn't find a doorbell, so Jinx knocked on the gate. A little door, set in the lower half of the left-hand gate, swung open and a woman in uniform stuck her head out. "Yes?" she said.

"We're here to visit a prisoner," said Jinx.

"Do you have an appointment?" asked the prison warder. (They called them warders, not guards, at Langley Women's Prison.)

"No, madam," said Rodders Lasenby, "we do not. Is that a problem? Are you going to make things difficult for us? I do respect a person in uniform who makes things difficult for us. It shows that they're earning their wages."

"No problem at all," said the warder. "Do you have any bags for me to search?"

"No," said Jinx.

"Would you like us to go and find some and come back with them?" asked Rodders Lasenby helpfully. (He was a big fan of luggage.)

"Not necessary," said the warder. "Go straight on in. Ask for her at the main desk."

"Thank you," said Rodders.

The warder stood aside and they stepped through the small door in the big gate to find themselves not in a courtyard but a big garden. In summer, some of the prisoners would probably have been gardening, with others chatting in groups, sitting on benches reading well-thumbed paperback books or simply staring up at the sky. As it was, there was just one prisoner in the snow-covered garden, wearing her prison-issue thick winter coat. She was also wearing a non-prison-issue, strictly-not-allowed, hand-knitted scarf. But prison officers steered clear of Bad Babs.

Bad Babs stood up and faced the four men. "What are you doing here?" Her voice was so deep that it wouldn't have been out of place coming from the mouth of a cartoon walrus. "And why are you dressed as a mangy bird?" she asked Twinkle.

"Because I like birds," said Twinkle. Simple as that.

Bad Babs nodded. The answer seemed to

satisfy her.

"Good afternoon, madam," said Rodders Lasenby. "This is Michael Jinx, brother of Mandy, one of the inmates here. We're off on an important – er – outing and were hoping to

ask Mr Jinx's sister to join us."

"Just like that?" asked Bad Babs (not that the men knew that she was Bad Babs).

"I've been told that it's very easy to escape from here as long as you do it between 9 a.m. and 8 p.m. and don't tell the warders," said Jinx, gearing up to start whining again.

"The warders aren't the problem," said Bad Babs.

"There's a problem?" asked Lord Bigg.

"Bad Babs's the problem," said Bad Babs.

"And who's she?" asked Rodders Lasenby.

"I am," said Bad Babs, which, as you know, was true.

"And why are you a problem?" asked Lord Bigg.

"I didn't say I was a problem," said Bad Babs. "I said that I was *the* problem."

When Mr and Mrs Grunt and Sunny finally got settled in their train compartment, Mr Grunt and Sunny sat next to each other on one bench seat – leaving a space between them – and Mrs Grunt sat on the bench seat facing them. She had Chocolate Biscuit beside her and Sharpie on her lap. There was a jolt and the train pulled out of the station. After a while, the ticket collector slid open the door to their compartment and stepped inside. His name was Sam Worth and he knew the Grunts from past experience.

There had been the time, back in the days that Clip and Clop were pulling the caravan, when the donkeys had eaten all the herbs in his window box then stuck their muzzles through his kitchen window and eaten:

- the flowers in the vase on the table
- the vegetables on his plate
- the vegetables on his wife's plate
- the tablecloth
- his wife's hairpiece
- his Sunday newspaper (which he'd kept for the crossword)
- a small cushion.

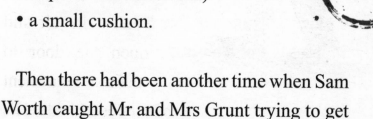

Then there had been another time when Sam Worth caught Mr and Mrs Grunt trying to get out of paying the fare to Steepleford Bendings by riding on the top of the train. To avoid falling off, they'd tried to fix themselves to the roof with some cheap glue. The glue had the consistency of stringy cheese on a pizza and smelled so strongly of fish that what first attracted the ticket collector to the train roof was the yowling of cats.

So when Sam Worth slid open the door from the corridor and said, "Tickets, please!" his heart sank when he saw who was occupying the compartment. "Oh, it's you," he said (which wasn't very polite). "Is it too much to hope that you have tickets?"

"We do," said Sunny, producing three singles to Hutton's Vale Halt out of a pocket in the front of his dress.

"Really?" said a stunned Mr Worth, taking the three tickets from the boy and studying them closely one at a time before lining them one on top of the other and clipping all three at once with his bright silver clipper to show that they had been checked. He handed them back to Sunny. "All bought and paid for?"

"Are you calling me a thief?" demanded Mr Grunt.

"Are you calling me a leaf?" demanded Mrs Grunt.

"Bay leaf!"

"Oak!"

"Birch!"

"Perch!"

"A perch isn't a tree. It's a fish!" said Mr Grunt.

"Who said anything about hats?" demanded Mrs Grunt.

"No one," said Mr Grunt.

"Precisely!"

"Picture frame!"

"Mud flap!"

Sunny cleared his throat. "Mr Peach from The Happy Pig bought us the tickets in advance," he told the ticket collector.

"Most *h*organised," said Mr Worth, who – unlike those people I referred to back in Chapter Three who liked to put "h"s on the end of words such as "mynah" – sometimes liked to stick "h" on the front of words such as "*h*opulent" and "*h*often", but only when speaking, not writing.

Satisfied that the Grunts had tickets, and relieved that they appeared to be behaving themselves but the teeniest bit sad that he didn't have an excuse to THROW THEM OFF HIS TRAIN, the ticket collector went back out into the corridor. He slid the door shut behind him.

"He looked very familiar," said Mrs Grunt.

"That's because he's our son," said Mr Grunt.

"Not the boy in the blue dress. The man who looked at our tickets."

"Then say what you mean," said Mr Grunt. "Now, let me get some sleep." He picked up his itchy blanket and placed it over his head again.

They hadn't been gone much more than an hour and Sunny was already missing the sanity of Fingers, Clip and Clop, and, of course, Mimi too.

And in the very next compartment were Lord Bigg, Rodders Lasenby, Michael Jinx, Twinkle and one other, along with a parrot called Monty, who was calling them all "*Big Nose*".

"Why might you be the problem in us getting to free my sister, Bad Babs?" asked Michael Jinx in Langley Women's Prison, earlier that very day.

"Are you really that bad?" added Rodders Lasenby. "I've nothing against bad, of course. Bad is good, but if it slows us down—"

Bad Babs laughed. It was the kind of laugh an adult bull seal might make if it found something deeply amusing. "I'm not that kind of bad," she said. "I'm not the wrestle-you-to-the-ground or shoot-'em-dead kind of bad." Her deep voice reverberated around the prison garden.

"There's another kind of bad?" asked Lord Bigg, raising an aristocratic eyebrow.

"Sure there is," said Bad Babs. "Surely you've met people who are bad cooks, bad at DIY…"

"DIY?" said a puzzled Lord Bigg. He wasn't familiar with the term.

"It means Do It Yourself, Lord Bigg," said Jinx.

"Why would I want to do anything myself when a servant can do it for me?" said Lord Bigg.

"…bad at games—" Bad Babs continued, getting into her stride.

"Aha!" Rodders Lasenby interrupted. "Bad as in no-good-at! So you might just as well be called Useless Babs?"

Bad Babs's lower lip began to tremble.

"No offence!" Rodders Lasenby added hurriedly. "Some of my best friends are useless. It's a real skill."

Jinx, who seemed to be feeling the cold more than the others, had his hands in his pockets and was stamping his feet. "So what does you being useless have to do with us not being able to see my sister?"

Bad Babs looked embarrassed. "Well, you'll be able to see her but, at the same time, *not* see her," she said, which was confusing to say the least.

"You're not making a great deal of sense, Bad Babs," said Rodders Lasenby. "I do like a riddle."

"You'd better follow me," said Bad Babs.

"Finally!" said Jinx.

The four men followed the woman across the snowy prison garden and through a door marked "NO ENTRY". The handle came off in Bad Babs's hand. It was apparent that she was even bad at opening doors.

They found themselves in a long, wide corridor with various numbered open doors leading into cells on either side. On seeing Bad Babs, some of the prisoners – who were all women and all wearing powder-blue jumpsuits – stopped chatting to each other and hurried back into their rooms.

Bad Babs turned to say something to Lord Bigg and the others, and tripped over her own foot. She grabbed the nearest thing to steady herself. It was a wall-mounted fire extinguisher, which came off the wall, hit the floor and started spraying water everywhere. A couple of now-soggy inmates let out a squeal and dashed for cover.

At the end of the corridor, they turned left, passing beneath a sign marked:

H SP T L W NG

"It should say 'HOSPITAL WING'," Bad Babs explained, "but Tilly Morton stole all the vowels. That's why she was sent here in the first place – vowel theft – but it hasn't cured her of the habit."

"Is she the person responsible for the Overton Opera House sign being an unreadable mess?" asked Rodders Lasenby. (The last time he'd passed the opera house, in his sleek motor car, Sweet Lizzie, it had read: "V RT N P R H S", which wasn't very helpful.) "I do so appreciate creative vandalism."

"Yes, that was Tilly's handiwork," said Bad Babs.

"Hospital wing?" said Michael Jinx. "My sister is in the hospital wing?"

"Yes," said Bad Babs. They stopped outside a door that had a small whiteboard fixed to it. On it, in thick black pen, was written:

Michael Jinx pushed the door open and was the first inside. When he laid eyes on the figure lying in the hospital bed he realised at once what Bad Babs had meant when she'd said that he'd be able to see Mandy but at the same time *not* see her.

Bad Babs led them right over to the bed, on which lay Mandy completely covered in bandages from head to toe.

Michael Jinx let out a whimper like a puppy with a trodden-on tail.

Chapter Six

On the Move

Mimi was worried. She was worried that if the escaped prisoners came looking for the Grunts in the grounds of Bigg Manor and found them gone, they might not just kidnap Fingers or Clip and Clop but even Old Mr Grunt. So she made a decision. She went to see Lady "La-La" Bigg over in her pigsty.

Unlike the roof of Bigg Manor itself, the roof of the pigsty was free from snow. The reason was simple. It had been melted by heat escaping from the sty. Her Ladyship was giving Poppet, her pig, a hot bath. They were both inside because of the cold weather. The sty was nice and steamy and toasty warm.

"Hello, Mimi!" said La-La cheerfully. She was busy washing Poppet's back with a great big sponge.

"Hello, Lady Bigg!" said Mimi. Her glasses had misted over in all that steam. She took them off and rubbed the lenses with her thumb and forefinger. "I wanted to let you know what's happening."

"About what?" said Lady Bigg with a smile. "Go on, dear. Spit it out."

"Well, you know about Lord Bigg?"

"What about him, dear?"

"About him escaping from jail."

Lady "La-La" Bigg dropped the sponge in the bath with a *SPLOSH!*

"Oh," said Mimi. La-La Bigg obviously had

no idea that Lord Bigg had escaped from jail.

"When?" she asked, patting Poppet on the back in a distracted manner.

"Yesterday, I think," said Mimi. "A man from the prison came to see Mr and Mrs Grunt to warn them. A Mr Hindenburg."

"Warn them?" Lady "La-La" Bigg asked.

"Warn them that Lord Bigg and three other men he escaped with might be coming after them and Sunny and Mr Smalls."

Lady "La-La" Bigg looked through one of the small pigsty windows over to the house. The stonework around many of the windows was blackened by smoke, a reminder of past disasters. "I remember Mr Smalls," she said. "Poppet here had a *most* traumatic time … but why should my husband be after the Grunts?"

"Well, there were the fireworks, for a start," said Mimi. (Ah, the fireworks. That's another story.[6])

"That silly man has only himself to blame," said Lady Bigg. She fished the dropped sponge out of the soapy water and began washing her beloved pig again. "Heaven knows what poor Horace will think." (Horace being their son.) "Now, what did you want to tell me, dear?"

"I'm going to go away for a while in the caravan. I'll be taking Old Mr Grunt, Fingers, and Clip and Clop," Mimi explained. "I thought you should know, just in case."

"Just in case what, dear?" asked Lady "La-La" Bigg. "Rest assured, Mimi, if my husband comes here with any ideas about

[6] In a book called *The Grunts in Trouble.*

129

making trouble, then trouble he will get!"

"Apparently, one of the men who escaped with Lord Bigg is a bit of a thug," Mimi explained. "Do be careful."

"Don't worry about us, dear!" said Lady Bigg. The "us" she referred to were herself, Poppet the pig and the two remaining servants at Bigg Manor: Agnes the chambermaid and her husband Jack the Handyman/Handyman Jack. "Thank you for telling me."

Back outside, Mimi found herself shivering. The contrast between the temperature of the lovely warm pigsty with its snow-free roof and the cold outdoors was teeth-clattering.

Next, she found Fingers. He was happy for her to hitch him up to the caravan and to load the donkeys in their special trailer on the back.

Because it was snowy, she also made sure that both Clip and Clop had their donkey blankets over them. To tell the blankets apart, Mrs Grunt had written a large letter "C" on Clip's for "Clip", and a large letter "C" on Clop's for "Clop".

And no, I don't think that made a great deal of sense either but if that was what Mrs Grunt wanted to do, who was going to stop her?

Now with the animals ready and in position, Mimi was ready to take the Grunts' caravan up the long, overgrown drive of Bigg Manor and out past the snow-covered broken-down gateposts and on to the lane. Mimi had been a passenger aboard the caravan many times. She'd even been the driver but she'd never been out in it alone before. It felt strange.

But first she had to get Old Mr Grunt on board. She'd saved this part of her plan until last because she knew that it would be the hardest.

She found Old Mr Grunt in his shed, having a fight with a large nail in a piece of wood.

He hit the nail with a large hammer.

CLANG!

And the nail didn't budge a hair's breadth.

So he hit the nail again.

CLANG!

And rather than going straight in, the nail bent slightly.

So Mr Grunt hit the nail sideways, to try

to straighten it up before hitting it from the top again.

TINK!

But nothing happened so he hit it harder this time.

TUNK!

And now it had bent in the *other* direction.

So Old Mr Grunt was now hitting it from the other side to straighten it up again.

TINK!

All the while, Mimi was trying to explain about taking him, Fingers, Clip and Clop somewhere safe. And all the while he was huffing and puffing or grunting with each *CLANG! CLANG! TINK! TUNK!* and *TINK!*

"Don't worry about me," he said at last.

"But I do worry," said Mimi. "If Sunny had had time to think I'm sure he wouldn't have wanted to leave you here."

Old Mr Grunt dropped the hammer, turned to Mimi and said, "Can I bring Maisy?"

"Of course you can," said Mimi without stopping to consider who or what Maisy may be. She'd never even *heard* of Maisy.

Old Mr Grunt rummaged under his workbench and pulled out an enormous cuddly owl. Much loved and very grubby, it appeared to be made from an old vest, with button eyes. Old Mr Grunt clutched it to his chest.

"Let's go," he said.

Jinx, Bigg, Lasenby and Twinkle stood round the hospital bed on which lay the totally bandaged-up Mandy. Bad Babs stayed in the doorway.

"What happened to you, sis?" Michael Jinx gasped.

"She was working in the prison laundry," said Bad Babs behind them.

"And?" asked Lord Bigg, raising one of his aristocratic eyebrows.

"I was pushing along a laundry basket and accidentally knocked her into one of the industrial washing machines."

Michael Jinx's eyes widened in horror.

"It took forty-five minutes to get her out," Bad Babs continued. "The doctor said he'd never seen a patient so clean."

"Is she in pain?" asked Jinx, glancing from Mandy to the guilty-looking Babs.

"The prison doctor seems to think she's numb all over, and that under all those bandages she has very soft skin smelling of spring meadows. Something to do with the fabric conditioner."

Rodders Lasenby was impressed. He was sure the laundry back at Stonewell Jail didn't use fabric conditioner.

"How long do you think she'll be all mummified?" asked Lasenby. "Not that she doesn't look good swathed in bandages. If anyone can make the covered-from-head-to-toe-in-bandages look work, I'd say your sister can, Jinx," he added.

"You'd have to ask the doctor that," said Bad Babs.

"Unfortunately, we can't stay around to ask anyone anything," said Lord Bigg. "We're on a tight schedule."

Michael Jinx leaned forward and gave a brotherly kiss to Mandy's bandaged forehead.

"Get well soon, Mandy," he said.

As he stood up, he could see her eyes staring up at him through the slit in the bandages.

"I agree," he said. "I could do with a false moustache."

"You could always use this," Bad Babs suggested. She held up the black marker pen that was attached by a piece of string to the whiteboard on the door, on which was written:

JINX, Mandy
636

She gave the pen a yank to try to free it from the board. Instead she somehow managed to pull the whole board from the door. It clattered to the floor and the string broke. She was left holding the pen, which she now handed to Jinx.

To tell the truth, all four men were a little in awe of Bad Babs. She was a one-woman walking disaster.

Jinx took the pen cautiously. "Thank you," he said. He looked at his reflection in a little metal mirror fixed firmly in place above a small hand basin and drew a thick black moustache on his upper lip.

Once satisfied with the result, he went over to the bed and drew a moustache on the bandages covering Mandy's upper lip. He went for the traditional ringmaster's look, with twirly ends.

"There you go, sis!" he said.

Rodders Lasenby looked at his wrist where his watch would be if he wore one. "We'd better go," he said.

They had just reached the door when, to their and Bad Babs's amazement, they heard a grunt behind them and turned to discover Mandy swinging herself up and off the bed.

She looked like a come-to-life Egyptian mummy in a scary film.

"Um umming wi woo," she said through muffled bandages: *I'm coming with you.*

"You can walk!" said Bad Babs in amazement.

"Mummified Mandy," muttered Lasenby under his breath.

Chapter Seven
Camera Action

Speedy McGinty had a number of wheelchairs for a variety of purposes. Her favourite was a lightweight one, made from chrome-coated aluminium. It wasn't her most comfortable chair but she could move around in it – even spin around in it – at a fair speed, and it was more comfortable than some of the stripped-back racing ones.

She was sitting in this chair while she nervously awaited the arrival of Sunny and the Grunts. She was worried. In her opinion, her bungalow might not be the most sensible place to hide. That dreadful Rodders Lasenby was only too familiar with her (as those of you who've read *The Grunts All at Sea* will know), as were the Jinxes, who even knew where she lived. Might it not be better if the Grunts went somewhere where they weren't known at all?

But then again, wherever Mr and Mrs Grunt went, they weren't very good at blending in. When they'd been camping, they were the ones who accidentally set fire to each and every tent on the site when they borrowed some flaming juggling-clubs. When they'd tagged along with a bird-watching group, Mrs Grunt was the one who sat on the particular rare bird they were looking for. It was OK. It survived but it looked flatter and less happy than it would have otherwise.

And they did both shout a lot. And were such big fans of laughing and pointing. It's probably OK to laugh and shout at a rock out at sea or at a funny-shaped vegetable, but Mr and Mrs Grunt usually laughed at people. Sometimes they laughed and pointed at people who had done something that the people themselves might have been embarrassed about, such as dropping a plate or treading in a cowpat. And having the Grunts draw attention to them made it even *more* embarrassing. Then there were the occasions when Mr and Mrs

Grunt would laugh and point at people for no obvious reason. In a way, this could be just as bad because the poor laughed-at-and-pointed-at people were wondering WHY they were being laughed and pointed at. Had they done something silly without realising it? Did they have such a huge piece of food stuck between their front teeth that the weird-looking couple from over the road who were doing the laughing and pointing COULD ACTUALLY SEE IT FROM THERE?

So it's not difficult to see why Speedy McGinty had serious, serious, serious – that's three seriouses – doubts about the whole "Grunts lying low for a while" thing.

Another problem was that Mr Grunt was always reluctant to actually come into her bungalow. He usually spoke to her at the door or through an open window. Sometimes even through a closed window. The reason was Speedy's dog. Mr Grunt wasn't frightened of her dog in the sense that he thought that she – the dog's name was Petal – might do him harm. Quite the opposite, in fact. Petal was so tiny that he was worried he might accidentally stand or sit on her. (Back when he did come into the bungalow he once stood on one of her squeaky, squishy dog-toys. He mistook it for her and had never quite recovered from the experience. Say what you like about Mr Grunt – oh, go on! – but at least he liked animals.)

But if the Grunts wanted to hide out in her bungalow, she was too good-hearted to say no.

A dog had been on Twinkle's mind too. One very different from Speedy's little dog, Petal. Now that Jinx had Mandy, Twinkle decided that he wanted his dog. (If you have a good memory, dear reader, you may recall my mentioning the mutt back on page 10.)

"Now we get my dog," said Twinkle.

"Your dog?" said Jinx. "It'll probably shed hairs everywhere," he muttered.

"My dog." Twinkle nodded, glaring at Jinx (who was himself very hairy).

"Your dog?" said Lasenby. "Splendid! The more the merrier. Perhaps we could pick up a trained monkey while we're at it?"

"I remember your dog," said Lord Bigg. "Big teeth."

"Shark," said Twinkle. "He's called Shark."

"Well, once we've captured the Grunts you can get your—" began Jinx.

"BEFORE," said Twinkle.

"R-right," said Lasenby. "Before." Not one of them wanted to upset the big man in the bird suit.

"Actually, it's an excellent idea," said Bigg. "If the sight of our friend Twinkle here isn't enough to make the Grunts do exactly as we say, Twinkle with a snarling Shark will be sure-fire success."

"Great," said Jinx.

"Let's do it," said Lasenby.

So it was agreed. They would go to Twinkle's house and collect Shark, his snarly-bitey-don't-mess-with-me hound.

Once on the train, Bigg, Lasenby, Jinx and Twinkle were planning ahead. Jinx was feeling a lot happier since he'd drawn a fake moustache over his top lip and had Mandy with him. He looked over to her, all covered in bandages, sitting in the corner.

"So what happens once we have Shark?" asked Rodders Lasenby, leaning back in his seat in the railway carriage. He was peeling the shell off a hard-boiled egg, placing the pieces in a large white cotton hanky resting on his lap.

"We have the element of surprise on our side," said Bigg.

"But once we've nabbed them, how do we get to the place where the lovely big crate is waiting for them?" asked Jinx.

"I was thinking—"

Whatever it was that Twinkle was thinking would have to wait. The door from the corridor slid open and Sam Worth, the ticket collector, poked his nose in. "Tickets, please, gentlemen," he said. He looked at Lord Bigg with surprise.

"What is it?" asked Bigg.

"Oh, nothing. Forgive me, sir," said Sam Worth, who had recognised Lord Bigg

instantly and knew that he was supposed
to be in prison. He quickly came up with a
reason for looking uncomfortable. "It's just
that the Grunts are in the next compartment."
He nodded his head in the direction from
which he'd just come. "And as anyone who
knows the Grunts knows, where the Grunts
go, trouble's never far behind."

A look passed between the escaped
prisoners.

"The Grunts, you say?" said Rodders Lasenby.

"That's right. Mr and Mrs Grunt and their boy Sunny," said Sam Worth, who was now beginning to feel decidedly uneasy. The very large man dressed as a very large bird was now smiling at him in a very worrying way.

"Do you know who I am?" Lord Bigg suddenly demanded in a voice that would stand for no nonsense.

"No, Your Lordship," said Worth.

Uh-oh.

Your Lordship wasn't the best thing he could have said. It was like the time he had arranged a surprise birthday party for Mrs Worth and she'd come home and asked him why there were flowers on the mantelpiece. And he'd blurted out, "What surprise party?"

Lord Bigg glared at him.

Sam Worth sighed. "I mean, yes, Your Lordship. But ... but *h*aren't you – er – supposed to be in jail?"

Bigg looked at Lasenby. Lasenby looked at Jinx. Jinx looked at Bigg. Bigg looked at Twinkle.

And Twinkle?

Twinkle picked up the ticket collector before the poor man knew what was happening.

Mummified Mandy just sat there.

Less than five minutes later, poor Sam Worth found himself rolled up, tied up and gagged with some strips of old sacking they'd brought from the derelict garage. They laid him in the luggage rack above Lasenby's and Jinx's heads.

"The next compartment?" said Lord Bigg. "How *very* convenient!"

"*Big Nose!*" screeched Monty.

In their compartment right next door, Mrs Grunt was shuffling around uncomfortably at her end of the bench seat.

"How much longer?" she asked.

"Longer than what?" demanded Mr Grunt.

Mrs Grunt chose to ignore him.

Sunny was busy writing his name with his finger in the condensation on the window, his chin resting on his other hand. As I've said at *least* once before, Mr and Mrs Grunt weren't his birth parents. Mr Grunt had rescued him from a washing line from which he'd been hanging by his ears as a baby. He'd given him to Mrs Grunt as a present. But they'd brought him up the best way they knew how – weirdly

– and they obviously loved him. As for Sunny, all he seemed to remember about his birth parents were his father's highly polished shoes and his mother's angelic singing voice (though only one song about skipping little lambs that he could never quite remember the words or the tune of, however hard he tried).

Once he'd thought that Agnes the maid at Bigg Manor and her husband Handyman Jack (also known as Jack the Handyman) were his mum and dad. Then he'd suspected that his parents might be Lord and Lady Bigg. He was certainly pleased when *that* turned out not to be the case. Now all but a very small part of him had given up hope of ever discovering who his birth parents were, let alone meeting them. But that small part was like a tiny splinter in your thumb: small but not easily ignored or forgotten.

"I'm hungry," said Mr Grunt, removing the blanket from his head.

"And stupid," said Mrs Grunt.

"That too," said Mr Grunt, which surprised all three of them. "Do they sell snacks on the train?" He was more used to travelling on the roof or having been thrown off by now.

"There's a buffet carriage," said Sunny, "but we're supposed to be keeping a low profile, remember?"

"You could go and get the snacks," said Mrs Grunt, who was hungry too. "You blend in anywhere."

Sunny glanced at his reflection in the small mirror on the opposite wall of the carriage. He looked at his wonky ears – one much higher up than the other – and his incredible sticky-up hair. He thought of his blue dress. He didn't think the phrase "blend in" was very accurate.

"I think we should all stay in the compartment," said Sunny.

"Nonsense," said Mr Grunt. "We need snacks." Mr Grunt dug his hand in his pocket and produced a few coins, a squashed bottle top and a peanut in its shell. He ate the peanut and handed Sunny everything else, including the bits of shell. "You know what I like," he said.

What the Grunts and Sunny mainly ate was roadkill: animals run over or hit and killed by traffic and left squashed on the tarmac. It was a regular supply of free meat. Sunny didn't know whether they particularly liked it but it was what they ate. And he was pretty sure that he wouldn't be able to buy a squirrel sandwich or badger stew from the train's buffet car.

"I'll do my best," said Sunny.

Out in the corridor, he was adding up the

meagre change in his hand
when his calculations
were interrupted by a
worryingly familiar voice.

"...*and I may end up with
a grazed elbow or knee*..."

It couldn't be, surely?

"...*not that I'm not delighted at the thought
of a bit of rough and tumble.*"

But it was.

No one else talks like that, thought Sunny.

It's Rodders Lasenby!

The inner windows of the next compartment
had their blinds down but Sunny risked
peering through a gap at the side ... and almost
GASPED. It was indeed Rodders Lasenby
(without his pinstripe suit and salmon-pink
tie). And he was with Lord Bigg (without
the criss-cross of plasters all over his face

that Sunny was used to) and the man Sunny had known as Max (not with a stick-on but a drawn-on moustache), an ENORMOUS man in a worse-for-wear bird outfit and someone bandaged from head to toe. *THE VERY FOUR MEN WHO WERE OUT TO GET THEM WERE ON THE SAME TRAIN.*

Sunny ducked and hurried back to his own compartment, sliding the door shut behind him.

"That was quick," said Mrs Grunt.

"They're here," said Sunny urgently.

"Where?" said Mr Grunt, looking around for the snacks.

"Lord Bigg and the others. They're in the next compartment!"

"What?" demanded Mrs Grunt. Her jaw fell open like a pair of loose scissors. "Stop the train! I want to get off!"

"We should tell the ticket collector," said Sunny urgently. "Then he can get the driver to radio ahead and have the police waiting to arrest them at the next station."

"And risk being murdered in the meantime?" said Mrs Grunt. "No thank you very much!" She had struggled to her feet and opened the outer door to the compartment. The countryside whistled past in a blast of cold air.

"And where do you think you're going, wife?" asked Mr Grunt. "We're moving, you daft moon-boot. Go through that and you'll fall off the train and break your neck."

"What should we do then?" said Mrs Grunt, struggling to close the door.

"Do they know we're here? That's what I want to know," said Mr Grunt.

"Why else would they be on the train, Dad?" asked Sunny.

"Hmmm. Are you absolutely sure it's them?"

"Sure I'm sure."

"I want to take a look for myself," said Mr Grunt. Now he had got to his feet and was striding to the sliding door to the corridor.

"No, wait, Dad!" said Sunny with real urgency. "If they spot you we could be in deep trouble. For all we know, they're armed and dangerous."

"I will keep low and move with the stealth of a panther," said Mr Grunt, extremely proud of his (correct) use of the word "stealth".

"This is too risky," said Sunny. "Let me go and find the ticket coll—"

"I've made up my mind," said Mr Grunt somewhat grandly.

"And I've made up my make-up," said Mrs Grunt.

Mr Grunt frowned. "You're not wearing any make-up, woman!" he snapped.

"It's imaginary make-up," Mrs Grunt snapped back. "I told you I made it up."

"They could be dangerous," said Sunny. "How do we know they don't have accomplices? How do we know they don't have weapons? They've probably been mixing with hardened criminals in Stonewell Jail. That Twinkle looks terrifying. He's huge, Dad."

"It's a risk I'm prepared to take!" said Mr Grunt. He was looking around for a makeshift weapon of his own, just in case he was spotted. He was about to grab Mrs Grunt's cat-shaped doorstop, Chocolate Biscuit, but she beat him to it.

"Oh, no you don't," she said. "If you're going to take a peek at them to see if Sunny's

159

got it right, then I'm going to take a peek to see if *you* got it right. And I'm taking Chocolate Biscuit for protection." She thrust her stuffed hedgehog into her husband's hand, spikes first. "Here," she said. "Use Sharpie."

Sunny really didn't think this was a very good idea at all but he wasn't going to be left behind and risk letting Mr and Mrs Grunt take everything into their own hands …

… which is how Mr Grunt with Sharpie in hand, Mrs Grunt with Chocolate Biscuit in hand and Sunny with nothing in hand came to be crawling down a railway carriage corridor

on their hands and niece. (Sorry. That should be nephew. I mean knees: hands and *knees*.)

"They're in there," said Sunny, mouthing the words and pointing up at the inner door and windows to the compartment.

Mr Grunt lifted his head to peer through a crack in the blind.

Apart from a very angry ticket collector bound up with sacking on the luggage rack and a splash of parrot poo slap bang in the middle of the floor, the compartment was completely empty.

Chapter Eight
A Change of Direction

What Mr and Mrs Grunt and Sunny didn't know was that just as they were sneaking down the train corridor ready to peer into their compartment, Bigg, Lasenby, Jinx, Twinkle and even mummified Mandy were making their way along the *outside* of the train ready to burst through the outer door of the Grunts' compartment. So each group ended up in the other's compartment wondering where the others had gone.

If you were wondering what Lord Bigg,

Rodders Lasenby, Michael Jinx, Twinkle and mummified Mandy looked like clinging to the side of the train, here's an illustration:

Mrs Grunt was still waving her cat-shaped doorstop in the air, despite the fact there was no sign of the enemy. Sunny and Mr Grunt, meanwhile, helped Sam Worth down from the luggage rack and out of his bonds. The ticket collector rubbed the back of his head as he sat up on the floor of the compartment.

"Thank you," he said. "You'll never believe—"

"Lord Bigg?" asked Sunny.

"Why, yes," said Sam Worth. "*H*and I thought he was supposed to be in jail."

"He escaped," said Sunny. "And he's after us."

Mr Worth looked from Sunny to Mr and Mrs Grunt and back to Sunny. "He's *h*after you?"

"Revenge. He wants to get his own back," said Mr Grunt, scowling at his wife.

"To front," said Mrs Grunt.

"To front?"

"Back to front *and* the wrong way round," said Mrs Grunt.

"Stop your nonsense!" said Mr Grunt.

"Stop the train!" said Mrs Grunt …

… and she pulled the communication cord. This rang a bell in the engine driver's cab and he slammed on the brakes for an emergency stop.

There was a screech of metal as the locked wheels moved down the track, sending up a spray of sparks and throwing everyone forward, followed by silence as the train stopped, now throwing everyone backwards.

Sunny flailed his arms around like an octopus juggling invisible balls, his heart in his mouth, as he tried to hold on to something. Anything. He let out a "Whooooooaaaaaa!"

Mr Grunt grabbed on to Sam Worth and in that brief moment they looked like a pair of skaters trying to remain upright on the ice.

Mrs Grunt had the advantage of actually

holding on to something before the driver even put on the brakes: the communication cord that she'd pulled to stop the train. Unfortunately – foolishly, even – she let go.

A deafening silence followed.

"Wow!" said Sunny, getting to his feet. He felt a bit like the time he'd been in the open cockpit of an aeroplane during a loop the loop. His tummy felt stuck in his throat.

In their new compartment, the Grunts, Sunny and Sam Worth had all ended up in a heap, half on, half off one of the bench seats, with Chocolate Biscuit on top and – unfortunately for him – with Sharpie the hedgehog wedged under Mr Grunt's tummy.

Being stabbed by Sharpie didn't hurt as much as Monty's biting of Prison Officer Pinkle. It didn't hurt as much as the time that squirrel bit Mr Grunt's nose. But it did HURT.

"What did you go and do THAT for, wife?"
demanded Mr Grunt.

"I told you," she said. "I want to get off."

Sunny got to his feet and picked up the ticket
collector's cap, handing it back to him. Sam

Worth pushed it back into shape, put it on his head and pulled it into position with its peak.

"I'd better go and check *h*on the *h*other passengers," he said, dashing out of the compartment on slightly wobbly legs. He ended up comforting:

- a sobbing major
- a priest with an attack of the giggles
- a very posh lady with her head stuck in a stranger's hat box
- a tourist trapped under a pile of rucksacks
- a bicycle
- and...

Well, you get the picture. Mrs Grunt pulling that cord had caused chaos.

Five passengers – and a bird – who the ticket collector *didn't* encounter on the train were the escaped prisoners. Having found the Grunts' compartment empty, they had decided to go back to their own. They could have walked back via the corridor but chose to go back the way they came: on the *outside* of the carriage. And that's where they were clinging when Mrs Grunt pulled the communication cord and the train came to a sudden halt.

All five lost their grip and were thrown backward from the train with cries of real terror.

Luckily for them, they landed in a large hedge lining the railway track. I say luckily because although it was quite a scratchy, prickly hedge it broke their fall, cushioning their landing before they rolled into a convenient snowdrift.

Lord Bigg came out of it worst. Since Monty had been freed from his cage he'd pecked his master on the face a few times (for old times' sake), but after his unexpected meeting with a hedge Lord Bigg's face was now very scratched indeed. He'd also hurt his elbow.

Rodders Lasenby had a big tear in the left knee of his prison-issue trousers but otherwise looked and felt as right as rain. (And what's right about rain I have no idea, unless it's the answer to the quiz question, "What do you call that wet stuff falling from the sky?") Twinkle simply grunted and stood up. Michael Jinx was the one most shaken by the experience, which was a bit surprising because it had been his idea to enter and leave the compartment on the outside in the first place "for the element of surprise". But what had shaken him up most was what he'd just put Mandy through.

Here was a woman who, according to Bad Babs, had spent more time in an industrial washing machine than was good for you – in other words, any time at all – and in all his excitement he'd made her risk her neck again.

Mandy lay on her back in the snow, arms and legs outstretched, looking impressively like a stunned starfish.

"Are you OK, sis?" asked a very worried Jinx.

She raised her head and nodded.

He gave a sigh of relief.

Lord Bigg, already upright, was nursing his injured elbow. "I think we all came out of this rather lightly," he said.

"These trousers look a dreadful mess," said Rodders, playing with the torn flap of trouser over his knee. "Quite the latest fashion. Marvellous."

"Duck," said the bird-mad Twinkle.

"What's that, old chap?" asked Lasenby.

"Duck," said Twinkle.

Lasenby, Jinx and Bigg looked around for any sign of a duck. Or any bird, come to that.

"Out of sight," said Twinkle, crouching down behind the hedge. "Duck out of sight."

"Aha!" said Bigg, bending down beside him. "I get your meaning!"

The escaped prisoners hid themselves

behind the hedge.

"I wonder why we stopped," said Rodders Lasenby. "I do love a mystery."

"Maybe someone other than the ticket collector recognised us and called the police," whined Jinx. "Just our luck."

"Then the police would simply be waiting to arrest us at the next station," said Bigg. "There'd be no need to stop the train."

"Then what?"

Bigg shrugged. "Who knows?"

At that moment one of the outer doors, facing the hedge but further down the track, swung open. Mrs Grunt's head popped out. It started to snow again. (Not her head,

173

of course. That would be RIDICULOUS.)

"I really think we should stick to the plan, stay on the train and go to Speedy McGinty's, Mum," said Sunny.

"Not with those bad men about," said Mrs Grunt, looking out through the open doorway with Chocolate Biscuit tucked under her arm. "If we're on the run, we should do some running."

"You're right, wife," said Mr Grunt. "If they knew we'd be on the train they may even know where we're planning to go."

"And *how* did they know we were on the train, huh?" said Mrs Grunt. Her eyes narrowed with suspicion. "Answer me that!"

"A spy," said Mr Grunt. "One of us is a spy feeding information to the enemy! And I know it's not me, which means..." He glared at Mrs Grunt.

"And I know it's not me," said Mrs Grunt. "Which means…" She glared at Mr Grunt.

"Why would either of you be spies?" asked Sunny. "We're all in this together."

They both turned and looked at Sunny.

"He started it," said Mrs Grunt.

"Didn't," said Mr Grunt.

"Did."

"Didn't."

"Did. Did. Did."

"Didn't. Didn't. Didn't."

"Liar."

"Money box!"

"Pig iron!"

"Coat hanger!"

"Slow loris!"

"Ski pole!"

OK, so we know how Lord Bigg and the

others knew that the Grunts were in the next compartment – Sam Worth, the ticket collector, had told them – but how did they know that the Grunts would be on that particular train at that particular time? Were the Grunts right? *Was* there a spy in their midst?

Are you ready for the answer?

Are you sure?

How had they known?

The answer is that they hadn't.

H-A-D N-O-T.

Does that come as a surprise?

Well, it surprised me, and I'm the one telling this story.

You see, the thing is, they were well aware that the Grunts were shouty, loud and kicky. It wasn't as if they could simply say to them, "Please get in that large crate marked 'TO THE MIDDLE OF NOWHERE'," so that's why they were more than a little pleased to have Thomas "Twinkle" Winkle with them.

Yes, admittedly they were all four more than a little frightened of him themselves – Bigg less so because he saw Twinkle as a fellow bird-lover – but he was a VERY useful "bit of muscle" when it came making the Grunts do what they didn't want to do. And Twinkle PLUS Shark, his snarly-bitey-don't-mess-with-me hound, would be doubly threatening. And that's where they were heading: to Twinkle's house to collect the dog. And where was Twinkle's house? Why, in Neep, which was on the selfsame railway line as Hutton's Vale Halt, where Sunny and the Grunts were heading.

It was a complete and utter coincidence that they were on the same train at all.

Chapter Nine

New Recruits

"What does your aviary look like?" Rodders Lasenby asked Twinkle, still crouched between the hedge and the snowdrift by the railway track. "Does it have a huge cage made of netting, ruining a perfectly decent back garden? I do so enjoy seeing a perfectly decent back garden ruined. A rare talent."

"Yes," said Twinkle. "Why?"

"Is that it over there?" Lasenby was pointing to a row of cottages. Their back gardens backed on to a hedge-lined field that led down to the railway track. One of the gardens was completely covered in netting about eight metres high.

Twinkle's huge face broke into a smile.

That was indeed his aviary.

Lord Bigg gave a beaky grin. "By golly, you're right, Lasenby! The train must have been due to pull in to Neep Station in a matter of minutes. Come on!"

After Twinkle's arrest for stealing all those rare birds' eggs, the police and the APB – Animal Protection Bureau – were convinced that he had the one egg they *hadn't* been able to find hidden away somewhere in a nice warm incubator, ready to hatch. They'd searched every inch of his house and aviary, but found nothing.

The APB had been keeping an eye on his wife, Winnie Winkle, who'd been looking after the birds for the few weeks he'd been in Stonewell Jail, but she'd never led them to the precious egg.

Breaking cover, the five escaped prisoners dashed across the snow-covered field towards Twinkle's cottage. Well, four of them dashed and the fifth – Mandy – followed as best she could, bandaged from head to foot. Monty had chosen her shoulder to perch on.

No one on board the train spotted them, or, if they did, they didn't give them a second

thought. They were all too busy trying to get themselves and their luggage back to some sort of order after their unscheduled stop. Mrs Grunt and Sunny had even shut the carriage door again.

Under any other circumstances, Sam Worth might have been VERY ANNOYED with Mrs Grunt for pulling that stop-the-train cord. But he was far more annoyed that some escaped prisoners had chosen HIS train to climb aboard in order to get up to mischief and had bound and gagged him. And now he couldn't find them anywhere. Were they hiding or had they abandoned ship, he wondered.

Satisfied he'd done what he could to help his passengers as he passed through the carriages to reach the driver in his engine cab, the ticket collector then spoke to the driver, who radioed ahead to Neep Station just down the line. He asked the stationmistress (Ms Hope) to inform the police about Lord Bigg and the others, which she did immediately.

The policeman charged with recapturing Lord Bigg and the others was a certain Inspector Barnaby Brown. Before he became a policeman, Barnaby Brown had been a successful boxer under the name Barney "The Bruiser" Brown. And it was this name that

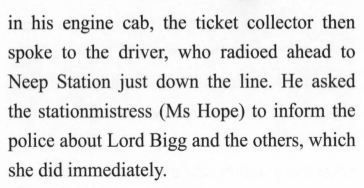

was embroidered on the back of a dressing gown once found in Lord Bigg's possession. In truth, His Lordship had quite innocently bought it from an Internet auction site, but because Lord Bigg had broken so many other laws and because he was wearing the dressing gown at the time and because it had been stolen and because Barnaby Brown was the arresting officer, Bigg was also charged with RECEIVING STOLEN GOODS: goods stolen from Barney "The Bruiser" Brown, no less. And now Lord Bigg had escaped and Inspector Brown was going to make sure that he recaptured him if it was the last thing he did.

And he had just been told that the escaped prisoners had recently been spotted on a train that had made an emergency stop just outside Neep. He picked up the large black phone on

his desk, pressed "3" and spoke into it.

"Sergeant Tooley? Bring the car round. We're going to Neep. And get me Officer Albany at the Animal Protection Bureau."

Just as Mr and Mrs Grunt had finally overruled Sunny's suggestion that they stay on the train and go to Speedy's as planned, the train started off again.

"Well, I'm not staying on until Hutton's Vale Halt," said Mrs Grunt. "I'm getting off at the next stop and running!"

"We don't actually have to run to be on the run, Mum," said Sunny for the umpteenth time. "We can let the train do the running for us … along the tracks."

"No, Sunny," said Mr Grunt. "For once in her life, the old nosebag is right. Lord Bigg and the others could still be anywhere on this train and pounce at any minute, like a coiled spring—"

"Or an uncoiled spring on a pouncing puma," said Mrs Grunt.

"What?"

"Nothing."

And then the train lurched and continued its journey.

No sooner had Sunny heaved a sigh of relief than the train pulled into Neep Station and Mr and Mrs Grunt spilled out on to the platform, thrusting Chocolate Biscuit (the cat-shaped doorstop), Sharpie (the stuffed hedgehog) and the string bag (full of clean underwear and melons) into Sunny's arms. Carrying the scratchy blanket, Mr Grunt marched out of the station exit, Mrs Grunt and Sunny close behind.

"What now?" asked Sunny. They were in a narrow country lane. There wasn't so much as a car park, let alone any houses – any other *buildings* – in sight.

"We go this way!" said Mr Grunt, striding purposefully to the right.

Mrs Grunt turned left. Sunny chose to follow her simply because that was the direction in which the train had been travelling. Mr Grunt grunted, but turned and followed them without a word.

It was mid-afternoon by now.

"It'll be getting dark soon," said Sunny.

"If I close my eyes it's dark now," said Mrs Grunt, doing just that and falling into a ditch.

Mr Grunt yanked her out. "Papoose!" he shouted.

"Compost!" replied Mrs Grunt, brushing the snow off her outer cardigan.

"Wattle!"

Sunny sighed to himself again and left them to it, trudging silently alongside them.

Then he heard a dog bark. Maybe they were coming into the village and could find somewhere to stay for the night?

The dog barked again.

Sunny looked around to see if he could see where it was. It was close by, in a field over to his right on a leash being held by that enormous man in the bird outfit, the one he'd first glimpsed in the railway compartment.

And despite the distance, Sunny had no trouble in recognising the man's companions (except for that person covered in bandages he'd first glimpsed in the carriage)...

"You know you were keen to run?" Sunny said to Mr and Mrs Grunt.

"Yes."

"Well, I think now's the time, because Bigg and the others are heading this way and they seem to have a dog with them..."

The Grunts looked in the direction Sunny was staring.

"Bother that Thomas Winkle!" muttered Mr Grunt. "That must be Shark!"

"Shark?"

"The dog. The giant in the bird costume is Thomas Winkle – Twinkle. We've had a few differences over the years."

"So, you *know* him, Dad?"

"I'm afraid so, Sunny. I once sold him a rare egg and it was neither."

"Neither what?"

"Neither rare nor an egg. My old da had made it out of clay and painted it. It looked very rare and very eggy."

"Oh," said Sunny. "You haven't upset any ancient Egyptian mummies too, have you?"

"No, why?" said Mr Grunt, as though it was a perfectly reasonable everyday question.

"Doesn't matter," said Sunny. "Let's go through here." They'd reached a gap in the hedge leading to a field on the opposite side of the road to the one the others were bounding down.

"Good idea!" said Mr Grunt.

"But all they have to do is follow our tracks," said Mrs Grunt, which was a bit of a surprise.

"That's true," said Sunny, impressed. "But they still have to catch up with us, so the bigger the distance we put between us, the longer it'll take them."

"Why don't we put our shoes on backwards, then they'll think we're going the other way?" said Mr Grunt. "Ha! That'll fool 'em."

"But if we were going the other way, we'd run into them."

"Mum has a point," said Sunny. "Sort of. Let's just get running."

So run they did.

"It's not easy in these," said Mrs Grunt, looking down at her bunny slippers. The snow showed up just how un-white they were.

The biting-cold air filled their lungs as they gathered speed in their escape, making breathing more painful. They heard distant

cries behind them, caught on the wind.

"There they are!"

"I say! Jolly good! We'll soon have 'em!"

"That'll teach them to throw tyres!"

"Uuy uunt we luum alln!" [7]

"Woof!"

Sunny spotted something up ahead, on the brow of the hill. It was a small herd of cows. Their field was still snowy but it had been cleared in places and some feed had been scattered on the ground.

"Let's head for those cows!" said Sunny, changing direction. Mr Grunt ran alongside him with Mrs Grunt following at the rear.

"Why?" she panted.

Shark barked again somewhere behind them. Closer now.

"We may be able to lose our footprints among theirs!" said Sunny.

[7] Or some such mumbling through bandages.

"We could hide in that building!" said Mr Grunt, pointing to the snow-covered roof of a barn that was coming into view as they ran up the hillside.

"Yeah," scoffed Mrs Grunt. "Like they won't think to search the one building for miles around."

"Apple-corer!" shouted Mr Grunt.

"Flea collar!"

"Finger food!"

"Pigeon loft!"

"Tr—"

"Mum. Dad," said Sunny. "Save your energy! Just keep running!"

They carried on up the hill as fast as the snow, their legs and lungs would let them.

Sunny was running out of ideas. If only Lord Bigg and the others didn't have that dog with them. They might be able to trick or confuse humans by hiding their footprints or mixing them up with others, but they couldn't fool a dog's nose. Its great big teeth were a concern if it caught them, but it was the animal's sniff-them-out nose that Sunny feared most.

They'd nearly reached the cows. All but one of them had their heads raised and were watching the oncoming Grunts with a mildly interested look in their big soft brown eyes. They were chewing winter feed like bored teenagers chew gum.

"What are they looking at?" said Mrs Grunt.

"Your ugly mug," said Mr Grunt (who, by the way, thought Mrs Grunt was very beautiful but wasn't about to admit *that*).

At last they reached the cows. One or two ambled away a short distance but most stood their ground.

"Now what?" said Mrs Grunt.

"We get inside the barn," said Mr Grunt.

Sunny was about to suggest they keep going, when Mr and Mrs Grunt ran inside. He followed, now wondering if there anything in there to help them with their escape. The barn was on two levels. There was a hayloft reached by a ladder, which after a quick inspection Sunny discovered was half filled with bales of hay. There were also piles of empty blue plastic sacks. It was surprisingly warm inside the barn. Perhaps the hay acted as a kind of insulation.

Downstairs, at ground level, was plenty of straw and a single bunny rabbit. Yes. A bunny rabbit. Perhaps he was a wild one that had wandered in for warmth.

(Don't sensible bunnies stay down in their burrows for winter?) Anyway, it was instantly obvious that this wasn't a sensible bunny because he took one look at Mrs Grunt's left bunny slipper and fell head over heels in love with it. He then took one look at Mrs Grunt's *right* bunny slipper and hated it on sight. Here was a rival for the affections of the bunny slipper he loved!

There was a hole in the side of the barn, which at first glance appeared to have a top row of very jagged teeth. They were, in fact, icicles. The Grunts peered through for signs of their pursuers.

Shark barked. Closer still.

"What now?" said Mrs Grunt, who was trying to shoo away the lovesick bunny with her foot.

"We could try starting up that tractor I found hidden under that tarpaulin," said Mr Grunt with a shrug.

"What? When? Where?" asked Sunny, looking around in amazement.

"You were up in the loft," said Mr Grunt, striding over to a dark and cobwebby corner.

"And you didn't call us over straightaway, Dad?"

"You're a complete and utter butter bean," said Mrs Grunt.

"Choking hazard!"

"Fly tip!"

"We don't have time for this!" said Sunny. "The others could be here any minute!" He wished Mimi were here. He could do with her brains and her company.

Sunny and Mr Grunt pulled the tarpaulin off the rest of the tractor. Mrs Grunt, meanwhile, was still having bunny trouble.

"There's no key in the ignition," said Sunny.

"Given enough time I might get it started if there's fuel in the tank but time's something we haven't got," said Mr Grunt. "I have an idea." He snatched a large spanner – an ENORMOUS spanner – hanging from a rusty nail on the wooden wall and began hitting the tractor's handbrake.

If there had been any doubts that the Grunts had been hiding in the barn, they would have been dispelled by now. Mr Grunt appeared to be announcing their presence with a drum solo.

"Jump up into the seat," Mr Grunt told Sunny. "You too, wife."

They both did as they were told. Mr Grunt went round the back and pushed. The tractor rolled forward.

"Shouldn't we have opened the barn doors first?" shouted Sunny.

"A bit late to think of that," said Mr Grunt. "Hold on tight!"

Sunny grabbed the steering wheel and held on SO tight that his knuckles – blue with cold – turned white.

Fortunately the old barn doors were not locked, simply closed, so when the front of the rolling tractor hit them one swung straight open with a judder and the other – more reluctantly – after only a little splintering of wood.

When Shark bounded snarling into the barn just a few moments later, closely followed by Twinkle-the-giant-bird and the others, all three Grunts were on the tractor

freewheeling halfway down the other side of the hill.

"Wheeeeeeeeeeeeeeeeeeeeeeeeeeeeee!" cried Mrs Grunt. She looked down to see the bunny rabbit clinging on to his rival, the right slipper.

"Good work, Dad."

"Thanks, Sunny."

"They're getting away!" cried Jinx.

Lord Bigg stared at him. "Did you really need to say that?" he snapped. "Is it really necessary to state the obvious? They have been getting away since the moment we spotted them on the train!"

"But I thought we'd caught up with them!" whined Jinx. "I really thought we had them this time!"

Mandy looked on in a *bandaged* kind of way but contributed nothing to the discussion. Monty was still sitting quietly on her shoulder.

"Stop whinging!" snapped Lord Bigg. He looked at Jinx as though he was a common criminal, which, of course, he was.

"I wouldn't worry too much about them being ahead of us for now," said Rodders Lasenby. He was still trying to catch his breath from running up the hill. "It's revenge we're after and it can't be much fun for them being chased by a ferocious hound. Adds to their punishment."

He bent down to pat Shark on the head but the dog gave such a dangerous-sounding snarl that Lasenby leaped backwards, jerking his hand back as though he'd just burned it.

"We need to get after them!" said Twinkle. "I have an idea."

Chapter Ten
A Cracking Time

At the bottom of the hill was a helium-filled balloon with a basket beneath it, tethered to the ground by a rope and anchor. In it stood a man. Imagine you were him. You're admiring the picturesque snow-covered scenery all around you when the doors of a barn at the top of the hill crash open and a tractor comes rolling out. There's a boy in a blue dress at the wheel and a woman behind him, arms round his waist like a pillion passenger on a motorbike. She is wearing a ridiculous elf-hat

203

and very grubby bunny slippers and appears to have a live rabbit grappling with her right foot. Running just behind the tractor is another strange-looking character who manages to jump up on the back of the machine before it gathers momentum and goes hurtling down the hillside STRAIGHT TOWARDS YOUR BALLOON.

But that's not the strangest thing. Wait a few minutes and you'll see four grown men and a mummy sledging down the snowy hillside on

four blue plastic sacks. (The mummy and one of the men are sharing a sack.) Three of the sacks are moving at quite a speed but one of them – ridden by an ENORMOUS chap in a grimy bird suit with a dog on his lap – seems to be too heavy and grinds to a halt. As the others sail down the slope, he has a change of plan. In next to no time, his blue-plastic-sack sledge is being pulled by the dog, who's loving it!

And at the bottom of the hill?

The tractor has, fortunately for you, missed your balloon and is heading straight for a frozen lake... *That's* what the man saw.

"Jump!" shouted Mr Grunt, and Sunny jumped. He was going to anyway. When you're on a tractor that is about to plunge into an icy lake, it seems the most logical thing to do. Mr Grunt jumped too.

Both of them landed on the snowy ground and rolled to a halt. Mrs Grunt still held on tight.

"Jump, you silly trench coat!" Mr Grunt shouted to his wife as he frantically scrabbled to his feet.

It was only as the front wheels of the tractor broke through the ice on the surface of the lake that Mrs Grunt plucked up enough courage to jump. She managed to fling herself on to the snowy bank but her left bunny slipper went flying up into the air. It landed and skittered across the ice, disappearing into the hole created by the tractor, which was now disappearing from view in a sea of bubbles.

The real, live bunny rabbit – who'd clung on to Mrs Grunt right up until the moment she'd hit the ground – lolloped to the water's edge and, without a moment's thought for his own safety, dived in to save the love-at-first-sight left slipper.

Sunny and the Grunts watched in awe as the animal came back to the surface, the slipper in his mouth, held in place with its impressive

two front teeth. Mrs Grunt put on the soaking-wet, freezing-cold slipper with one hand and held the soaking-wet, freezing-cold shivering bunny with the other. She kissed him.

"My hero," she said, slipping him inside her cardigans to warm him up. "Why don't you ever do heroic stuff like that, husband?" she demanded.

"And why didn't you jump when I told you to?" demanded Mr Grunt.

"Quick!" said Sunny with more urgency in his voice than there is jam in the jammiest doughnut. "To the balloon!"

"Which balloon?" asked Mrs Grunt.

"*Which* balloon?" spluttered Mr Grunt, already running towards the tethered helium balloon. "As if there's a CHOICE of balloons, you chip-fryer!"

Mimi had decided that a good place to take the caravan would be to park it up alongside Jeremy's house. Jeremy used to work at Larry Smalls Circus (no apostrophe) and was fond of Fingers. Jeremy lived inside a fibreglass tomato that had once been a prop in a TV advertisement. It was very big for a tomato but very small for a house, but, then again,

Jeremy was very small for a man. When Mimi finally arrived – with an elephant pulling the Grunts' extraordinary home, she had been able to take shortcuts across fields rather than having to stick to roads all the time – she found the tomato almost entirely covered by a snowdrift.

She heard muffled cries.

"Is there anybody in there?" shouted Mimi, jumping down from the driver's seat. Frizzle and Twist twirled above her head as she moved.

There was another muffled cry and more banging.

"Give me a hand, will you, Fingers," said Mimi, unhitching him from the caravan. "I think Jeremy's trapped in his own home!"

Fingers didn't lend a hand but he did lend a trunk, swishing a pathway through the snowdrift, revealing Jeremy's front door. (The fibreglass tomato had no windows.) Very carefully and elegantly, the elephant reached the door handle with the tip of his trunk, turned it and pulled the door open.

Jeremy tumbled out into the snow, a most unusual shade of blue. He gasped for breath.

"I was running out of oxygen," he said. "Thank heavens you came along when you did, Mimi. Thank you ... and you, Fingers." He stood up and looked around. "Are the others inside?" he asked, nodding towards the caravan.

"Just Old Mr Grunt," said Mimi. "Are you OK?"

"I am now," said Jeremy, back to his normal colour.

"Sunny and Mr and Mrs Grunt are going into hiding," said Mimi, unhitching Fingers from the caravan and then walking over to the donkeys' trailer to check on Clip and Clop. "Rodders Lasenby and some others have escaped from prison and are after them. They need to lie low for a while."

"WHAT?" said Jeremy in disbelief. "You'd better come in."

It was beginning to get dark.

Down by the banks of the frozen lake, Sunny was already in the basket of the helium balloon, next to the startled man who'd watched events unfold around him. Alfred Gumby – that was the man's name – could see that the Grunts were in trouble and was busy untying the anchor while Sunny was trying to pull Mrs Grunt – and Mr Grunt was trying to push Mrs Grunt – into the balloon. Just as she landed head-first next to Sunny, bunny-

slippered feet in the air and live bunny in her coat, Shark caught up with them, sinking his fangs into Mr Grunt's bottom.

He howled.

Mrs Grunt uprighted herself and began pummelling the top of Twinkle's head with her fists. "Get that half-baked croc off my husband!" she yelled.

But the balloon was now free of its moorings and gaining height.

"Daaaaaaaaaaaaaad!" shouted Sunny, but there was nothing he could do.

"Take me down this instant!" shouted Mrs Grunt, now pummelling poor Alfred Gumby instead.

"I can't!" he said. Which was true. The only way was up.

Mr Grunt managed to stop yowling in pain long enough to yell, "Look after the old sponge bag, Sunny!"

The last thing Sunny wanted to do was abandon Mr Grunt in his hour of greatest need but he knew that, even if he could get the balloon back to the ground, they were no match for Twinkle, his dog and the others.

Looking down at the rapidly receding ground – that's clever-speak for getting further and further away – he witnessed Rodders Lasenby and Jinx reaching the bottom of the slope and helping Twinkle with their prisoner.

The light was really beginning to fade now. And Sunny didn't know what to do. "Thank you for rescuing us," said Sunny to the man, "but we need to rescue my father."

"You're a boy!" said Mr Gumby, clearly surprised.

"He knows that, you spoon!" said Mrs Grunt to Mr Gumby.

Sunny looked down at his blue dress. "Too complicated to explain now. Sorry," he said. He was too busy trying to work out what to do. If they went to get help they might lose track of Mr Grunt. If they didn't get help, then they were still outnumbered (if you counted Monty and Shark and the one in the bandages). "Are we anywhere near a police station, do you know?" he asked.

"I'm afraid not," said Mr Gumby, "and even if we were, that wouldn't make much difference. I couldn't get you there."

"Why not?" asked Sunny.

Mrs Grunt just glared at Mr Gumby.

"With a hot-air balloon, you can control the height it goes with bursts of hot air from a burner. The hotter, the higher. That way you can find air currents to take you in the direction you want to go. I know that much.

This is a helium balloon. The helium gas is sealed inside," said Mr Gumby, then added, "The name's Gumby. Alfred Gumby."

"Gumby?" snorted Mrs Grunt. "What kind of name is that?"

"I'm Sunny," said Sunny hurriedly. "This is my mum, Mrs Grunt. That's my dad down there."

The balloon was drifting upwards and sideways, though Sunny had no sense of wind. (Balloons are like that. Because you blow *with* the wind. You don't stand still with the wind blowing *against* you.) Down

below he could see what was, in fact, Twinkle's aviary in the bird-lover's back garden – with the ground completely covered in snow beneath the netting except for one area, which stood out like a black square in the twilight – but he had no idea that was what it was.

"So how do you make this thing go where you want it to?" asked Sunny in desperation.

"Apparently you control buoyancy and weight," said Mr Gumby, but he didn't sound confident.

"What does that mean?" asked Sunny.

"I'm not sure," Mr Gumby confessed. "I was simply waiting in the balloon for a – er – colleague. I've no idea how to control it."

"Let me out!" cried Mrs Grunt, throwing

her left leg over the side of the basket. This not only alarmed Alfred Gumby and Sunny but also the bunny, because Mrs Grunt was wearing the bunny slipper he loved on the foot over the edge.

This was what we call a far from ideal situation.

"Surely the heavier the balloon is, the lower it must go," said Sunny.

"But how do we make it heavier?" said Mr Gumby. "We can make it lighter easily—"

"By pushing you out," interrupted Mrs Grunt helpfully.

"Mum," said Sunny. "Mr Gumby saved us both. He would have saved Dad if he could have. He may STILL save Dad. He's on our side."

The balloon was still rising.

"So we can make it lighter and go higher

by throwing things out, but balloonists can't add weights to make their balloons go down or they'd have to magic them out of thin air. There must be another way."

"Burst the balloon!" cried Mrs Grunt triumphantly. And I mean triumphantly. She may not have had a sword, knife or dagger to stab the balloon. She may not have had scissors or shears. But she held up something high: her new sharp-toothed friend, the rabbit. "Bunny to the rescue!"

"Wait!" said Sunny. "I think you might be on to something, Mum! If we can release some of the gas from the balloon that should make it go lower."

"Imelda – I mean Miss Albany did say something about heat affecting the envelope," Mr Gumby recalled.

"Envelope?" said Mrs Grunt. "This is no

time to be sending letters!"

"That's what she called the – er – balloon part of the balloon, madam," Alfred Gumby explained. "She said in hot weather the envelope needs less helium gas to go higher than it needs in very cold temperatures such as these."

"And how does that help, you fish fork?!?" demanded you-know-who.

"I was just thinking out loud," said Mr Gumby.

"The more we understand this thing the better," agreed Sunny, staring up at the envelope. It had large writing on it, but he couldn't read it from the basket. "What's it for, Mr Gumby?"

"For?"

"Why's the balloon here? What does it have written on it?"

"It's an observation balloon," said Mr Gumby. "It's for looking down on things." He looked down at his feet on the floor of the balloon basket.

What it did actually say was:

AN EGG IS FOR LIFE NOT JUST FOR BREAKFAST

Mrs Grunt's eyes narrowed with suspicion. "And why are you waiting for a colleague in an observation balloon on a cold winter's evening, gum-boy? Answer me that!"

"Wait!" said Mr Gumby. "We've stopped rising!"

It was true. The balloon had indeed stopped gaining height but in the failing light the ground was too far below to be seen.

"There must be a way of letting out some of the gas," said Sunny. "A valve or something. That will get us down."

But that wasn't what ended up getting the balloon down at all. What got them down was Monty.

Chapter Eleven

A Strange Discovery

Balloon envelopes are very tough. They have to be. What if they're hit by a flock of geese or parachuting rats with baseball bats? (Not that the second example is very likely.) But no balloon envelope could stand up to the might of Monty's beak and claws.

Of course, Mr Gumby, Mrs Grunt, Sunny and the bunny had no idea that Monty had abandoned the mummified Mandy's shoulder and had flown up, up, up to blow a hole in their plans. Whether the parrot was on a mission for Lord Bigg or just felt like attacking the giant egg-thing in the sky, I've no idea.

The end result was the same: the parrot made beak and claw holes in the envelope, and gas leaked out, ripping the holes into tears, and the balloon – with everyone in the basket, except Bunny, hanging on for dear life – began plummeting to the ground.

"Aaaaaaaaaaaaaaaaaaaaaaaargh!" cried Sunny.

"Aaaaaaaaaaaaaaaaaaaaaaaaaaaargh!" cried Mr Gumby.

"Sponge baaaaaaaaaaaaaaaaaaaaaag!" cried Mrs Grunt.

The basket
jerked to
a halt, not
unlike the
train stopping
but even more
violently. For
a brief moment
Sunny felt as if he
were wearing his
shoes – one lace-up,
one slip-on – inside his
head.

They had been saved by an enormous statue.

Instead of the basket hitting the ground, the deflated envelope and ropes attaching it to the basket had got in a tangle with a statue, bringing the basket to rest eight or so metres above the ground.

That's not to say that the balloon's occupants weren't beaten, battered and bruised.

Mrs Grunt struggled to her feet, checked Bunny was all right then gave Mr Gumby a swift kick. "Your parking's even worse than Mr Grunt's when he parks our caravan," she muttered.

Sunny was leaning over the edge of the basket trying to work out how they could get down. It was far too far to jump safely. He found himself staring at an enormous pair of highly polished black shoes.

Paint, he realised. The statue must be painted. Glossy black paint to look like shiny black shoes.

What was this place they'd ended up in? The statue appeared to be in the middle of a courtyard. The far side of the courtyard was the outer wall of a building with a large door.

Above it was the lettering:

TH RN RY RPH NG FRBYS

Had Sunny met Bad Babs, he might have realised that the sign had fallen foul of Tilly Morton the vowel-thief but he'd probably still have been too busy wondering how to get down to think about it much anyway.

Just then the courtyard was flooded with electric light and the door opened. A tall, thin, yet surprisingly imposing figure of a woman strode out and across the cobbles. She was brandishing an enormous frying pan.

She stopped in her tracks when she saw the remains of the helium balloon hugging the statue.

"Hello?" she called. "Are you all right up there?"

"We're having a picnic!" shouted Mrs Grunt sarcastically.

"We're OK. No one's hurt," Sunny called back. "But we're not sure how to get down."

The basket shuddered and suddenly dropped another metre before the ropes snagged again.

"Whoooa! We may have to climb down the statue," said Mr Gumby.

"Do be careful," said the woman.

"I'm not climbing down that thing," Mrs Grunt protested. She certainly wasn't dressed for climbing. Those bunny slippers of hers wouldn't give her much grip.

"Mattresses!" shouted the woman.

"Toilet brush!" shouted Mrs Grunt.

"I beg your pardon?" said the woman.

"You started it!" yelled Mrs Grunt.

"If one of you gentlemen could climb down the statue and help me bring down some mattresses from inside, perhaps the lady—"

"My mother," said Sunny. "Mrs Grunt."

"Then perhaps Mrs Grunt could risk climbing down, knowing there'll be a soft landing should she fall."

"You're alone in the house?" asked Mr Gumby.

The woman was still clutching the frying pan. "Yes," she nodded. "But I am armed."

Sunny was already gingerly climbing out of the side of the basket pressed up against the statue's torso and beginning the long climb down the painted stone trouser leg.

He reached the cobbled courtyard with a sigh of relief. The courtyard had been cleared of snow but now that evening was drawing in and the temperature dropping, it was very slippery.

He looked back up at the statue. It was an enormous figure of a man, with head bowed, clasping a top hat. Sunny thought it strange to see a statue painted. He was used to them being plain stone. The man wore a black suit and a bright-red waistcoat to go with those shiny black shoes. His hair was sandy yellow, as was the large moustache covering his mouth.

But Sunny didn't stop to look around and wonder. Not only were Mum and Mr Gumby still stuck up in the balloon basket but Dad was in the clutches of an evil gang that included a thug in a bird suit, a mummified heaven-knew-what, and a snarly dog and bitey parrot.

He hurriedly followed the woman across the floodlit courtyard, through the open door and up a flight of stairs. He quickly explained about the escaped prisoners and the capture of Mr Grunt as she led him down a maze of corridors with stone-flagged floors, past an enormous and very old-fashioned kitchen.

"Well, you'll be safe here once we get the others out of the balloon," said the woman. "This place is like a fortress. We've only ever lost one of our number and that was when we let Absent-Minded Annie do the laundry."

"Can we call the police?" said Sunny urgently.

"That would be a miracle," said the woman. "We've no need of a landline here. Everyone

uses their mobile phones."

"Then can you use yours to call the police?" said Sunny with growing exasperation. "Please?"

"Oh, I don't personally have one, dear. But the others do. Except that they're all off on an overnight outing. I'm the only one here."

"So no phone," said Sunny.

"No phone."

"So no police."

"I'm sorry," said the woman, shaking her head. They reached a staircase and she led Sunny up it. Upstairs was very different to where they'd come in. The floors were carpeted and the walls brightly painted but what was most striking was the size of all the furniture.

Jeremy would love it here, thought Sunny. It was all half-size.

"What is this place?" he asked.

"This is the Ornery Orphanage for Boys," said the woman (which is what the lettering outside was trying to say but with missing vowels). "And I am Edna Ornery, granddaughter of its founder, Albert Ornery.

It was his trouser leg you just climbed down. The statue is of him."

"I see," said Sunny.

"This way to the mattresses. If we take them off the children's beds, they'll be small enough to push through the window. Now that these criminals have your father, what will they do with him, do you think?"

"Well, I don't think they're cut-throats or murderers," Sunny admitted, "though I'm not sure about Twinkle."

Miss Ornery raised an eyebrow.

"Thomas Winkle," Sunny explained. "He's a very large man with a very vicious dog. And another one of them is dressed from head to toe in bandages."

"If I hadn't just found you the way I found you, I'd be inclined to think that you were making the whole thing up!" said Miss Ornery.

"If only," sighed Sunny.

They had reached a dormitory of twelve child-sized beds. Two rows of six. Miss Ornery was ripping the bedclothes off the nearest one to free the mattress. Sunny joined her.

"Do you think they'll demand a ransom?" she asked.

Sunny couldn't imagine that. "I expect people would pay to keep Mum and Dad hostage rather than pay to get them released," he snorted. He looked around at his custom-built, child-sized surroundings.

"These should be enough," said Miss Ornery. They'd stripped the sheets off half the beds in the room. Between them, they carried the mattresses out of the dormitory to a window on the landing overlooking the courtyard. Sunny opened the window wide. Suddenly, music filled the air.

"What's happening?" he gasped.

"It's on a timer," said Miss Ornery as they heaved the first mattress up on to the windowsill. Sunny looked up and saw speakers set just below ceiling height. "It's playing in all the rooms," she said.

The hairs on the back of Sunny's neck stood to attention. They were as spiky as Sharpie's prickles.

The music was soft and dreamy. Then a woman's voice started to sing. She had the voice of an angel and she sang about fluffy little lambs shaking their fluffy little lambs' tails.

The music seemed to flood over Sunny, soaking into the pores of his skin and reaching his heart. His face radiated a warm glow. But there was also a tightening in the pit of his stomach.

He forgot about Mrs Grunt and Mr Gumby in the balloon. He forgot about his father being prisoner. He found his thoughts transported back to his earliest childhood memory.

This song.

Sung by *this* voice. Sunny looked out of the window into the floodlit courtyard.

He gazed down on to the first thing he'd seen when looking out of the basket after crash-landing.

He looked at the statue of Albert Ornery. He looked at the feet: two shoes painted with black gloss paint to look like the shiniest of leather.

Sunny's head was reeling.

Time slowed.

The song.

The polished shoes.

"Are you all right, dear?" Mrs Ornery asked kindly. "You look pale."

In Sunny's mind it had been his mother – his birth mother – who had sung that song. In his mind those had been his birth father's shoes …

… but what if…?

What if?

What was it Miss Ornery had said? "*We've only ever lost one of our number and that was when we let Absent-Minded Annie do the laundry.*"

Laundry? Hadn't Mr Grunt found him as a baby on a washing line?

"The mattresses," said Miss Ornery. "Hurry, we must push out the mattresses."

But Sunny's thoughts were elsewhere.

Chapter Twelve

Showtime

Now that Bigg, Lasenby, Jinx, Twinkle and Mandy had their first prisoner, in the form of a VERY grumpy Mr Grunt, they weren't precisely sure what to do next.

He was currently inside a large sack they'd salvaged from the tractor barn at the top of the hill, which was where they all were now.

What was keeping Mr Grunt quiet was:

1. He had his own socks stuffed in his mouth.
2. Shark was curled up on top of him outside the sack.
3. He was sleeping like a baby.

"It's a shame the other two got away," said Lasenby with a sigh, "but it makes it all the more exciting that we still have them to capture in the morning."

"We need sleep," said Twinkle. "You take the first watch. Someone's got to keep an eye on this Grunt."

"Why me?" whined Jinx. "I've got my sister to look after."

Both Twinkle and Shark growled at the same time.

"OK, OK," said Jinx. "I'll take the first watch."

The four men and the bandaged woman snuggled down as best they could. With a good roof, hayloft and hay, the men slept much better than they had in that garage the previous night. Had they really only been settling down there twenty-four hours earlier? So much had happened since then.

Mandy's beady eyes watched Twinkle through the slit in her bandages.

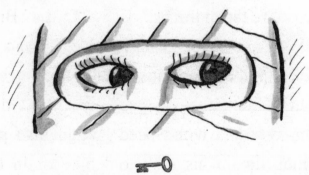

It was getting late and there was *still* no sign of the Grunts. Speedy McGinty was getting really worried now. She'd had enough of waiting. When the Grunts hadn't got off the (delayed) train at Hutton's Vale Halt, she thought that there might have been a change of plan. The problem was, the Grunts didn't have a phone. They'd never had one. Well, that's not strictly true. Mrs Grunt once owned a phone for about ten minutes before putting it in their fish tank (in the old television). It was silver-coloured and, she thought, almost fishy-shaped, and she decided that it looked pretty in among the fish. Lady "La-La" Bigg had no need of a phone in her pigsty and no one had one in the ruined Bigg Manor.

On the rare occasions that Mr Grunt communicated with Speedy rather than just turning up on his rusty old bike or in the caravan, he called her from a telephone box in the nearby village. That was how he'd arranged to hide out at her bungalow. But when there was still no sign of them hours after they were due to arrive, Speedy was getting really, really worried. If they didn't arrive by first thing the following morning she decided she would have to *do* something.

In the end, Mrs Grunt didn't even bother to try climbing down the stone trouser leg. She simply jumped on to the mattresses, laid two-thick, below. Mr Gumby waited for her to be helped to her feet and moved out of the way before he left the basket himself. Even though it wasn't his balloon and he'd had no idea how to fly it, he'd felt a bit like a captain of a ship: it was his duty to be the last off the stricken, stranded vessel. He managed to climb out of the basket and down the statue without incident.

Once inside it was agreed that Sunny and Mrs Grunt – and Bunny! – would stay safely

locked up inside the orphanage while Mr
Gumby went for help. Miss Ornery had urged
him to stay until morning but he felt time was
all-important.

With Mr Gumby gone, with a large torch,
spare batteries and a pork pie, a Scotch egg
and some grapes for his journey, Mrs Grunt
went to sleep on three of the orphans' little
beds pushed together.

Sunny sat with Miss Ornery in her private living room. She had given him a large mug of warming soup. "Miss Ornery?" said Sunny at last. They were both sitting in high-backed chairs, facing a small open fire.

"What is it, dear?"

"You know you said earlier that you'd only ever lost one person? Well, the person you lost… Was it a baby on a washing line?"

Edna Ornery looked flabbergasted. "How… How did you know?"

"Was it?" Sunny repeated. "Was it a baby on a washing line? Did this Absent-Minded Annie person hang a baby up by his ears to dry?"

There was silence but for the crackling of the fire.

Finally Edna Ornery spoke. "Yes," she said at last. "Absent-Minded Annie lives in the village and she used to come and help out at the orphanage as a volunteer. She loves children. We'd give her simple tasks and always under the supervision of a member of staff." She stared into the flames. "That day she was helping in the laundry while the laundry mistress was also looking after a little baby boy. The laundry mistress was only gone for a matter of minutes – to sort out a problem with a blocked tumble drier – and when she came back Annie had taken the baby out of the laundry room and hung him on the line."

"But when she went outside to look, he'd disappeared," said Sunny.

"Yes," said Miss Ornery. She turned and looked at Sunny. "I never saw him again."

"Liar!" bellowed Mrs Grunt. They'd both thought she was asleep but now she was standing in the doorway and nearly made them jump out of their skins.

"I beg your pardon?" said a startled Edna Ornery.

"You're seeing him right now," said Mrs Grunt.

"It's true," said Sunny quietly.

Edna Ornery looked from Mrs Grunt to Sunny to Mrs Grunt again. "You mean…? You mean…?"

"Yes," said Sunny. "That baby was me."

Tears sprang from Miss Ornery's eyes. She made a little choking sound.

"Dad – er – Mr Grunt rescued me from the washing line," Sunny explained.

"And we brought him up as our own," said Mrs Grunt. "He even has his own space on the landing."

"You're alive! You're well! You're wearing a blue dress…" Miss Ornery got up from her chair and gave the boy a great big hug.

Sunny had a thousand and one questions he
wanted to ask.

"When d—"

"Your questions will have to wait, Sunny," said Mrs Grunt, not unkindly. "You need to sleep." Sunny was about to protest when she added, "You'll need all your strength to help me get your dad back in the morning."

Sunny felt a pang of guilt. How could he be worrying about parents he couldn't even remember when the man who'd brought him up as his son was being held prisoner?

"Help you get your husband back?" said Miss Ornery. "I think we should leave that to the police."

"Oh, you do, do you?" snapped Mrs Grunt. "No one kidnaps my husband and gets away with it."

The next morning Sunny awoke to the smell of a proper breakfast being cooked. Not roadkill but NORMAL food. It smelled delicious. And despite his worries, he felt different. Today they would do everything to get Mr Grunt back AND he would find out more about his past. About where he came from. This was HUGE. This could be life-changing. But first things first.

He followed the mouth-watering smells to the kitchen, where Miss Ornery was standing by a large cooker, frying eggs in the selfsame frying pan that she'd been brandishing the day before. Mrs Grunt was already there, with Bunny on the kitchen table snuggled up next to her left bunny-slipper, which she'd plonked unceremoniously between pots of honey, jam and marmalade.

"Good morning, Sunny!" said Miss Ornery with a smile.

"Still no police?" asked Sunny.

"No," she said. "And no sign of your Mr Gumby either. I do hope he's all right. Sit where you like."

"Shouldn't we be *doing* something?" he said.

"Have some breakfast," said Mrs Grunt. "It tastes OK if you tread on it first."

"Sorry to break up the party," said a voice. There in the doorway stood Twinkle, his eagle suit now looking very much the worse for wear. He moved very quietly for such a big man.

Mrs Grunt was up and out of her chair and striding across the stone-flagged floor – one slipper on and one slipper off – without a moment's hesitation. She began pummelling

Twinkle. It had about as much effect as an ant punching a fairly large stone birdbath.

Rodders Lasenby and Michael Jinx appeared behind him now, far more noisily. Jinx was still glowing with pride at having been able to pick the big old lock of the orphanage's back door.

"How did you find us?" asked Sunny.

"The remains of the balloon we last saw you fly off in wrapped around that statue was a pretty big clue," said Jinx. He sounded happy for the first time in days.

"What have you done with my husband?" yelled Mrs Grunt. "If you've hurt so much as one of the horrible hairs on his idiot body—"

"Calm down, missus," said Twinkle, grasping her with both his enormous hands. "You'll be with him soon enough."

Sunny was thinking fast. There was no

sign of Lord Bigg, the mummified mystery or Shark the dog. They must be guarding Mr Grunt, wherever he was. So should they go quietly and be reunited, or try to make another break for it?

As soon as it was light, Speedy McGinty went to see her neighbour, Charlie Merrick.

"I have a favour to ask," she said.

"What is it, Speedy?" asked the bleary-eyed Charlie, who was still in her dressing gown. (Charlie was short for Charlene, and she was a she.)

"You know Mr Grunt, the man who sometimes comes to see me but won't come into the house?"

"The one who shouts at you through the window?"

"That's the one. Well, he may turn up with

his family. Can you keep an eye out for them and let them in if they do show up?"

"Of course," said Charlie.

"Thank you," said Speedy. She handed Charlie her spare key. "And – er – Charlie."

"Yes?"

"If anyone comes asking about them, you've never even heard of the Grunts. Right?"

"OK, Speedy."

"Thanks," said Speedy. She was wondering where on earth she should start looking for them.

Mimi and Old Mr Grunt had slept in the caravan but come breakfast time – having fed Fingers and the donkeys – Mimi planned to knock on the door of Jeremy's fibreglass tomato home to see if he wanted to join them for breakfast. She imagined Sunny with Mr and Mrs Grunt, safely lying low in Speedy McGinty's bungalow. How wrong she was. It was as Mimi was walking up the path that Fingers had cleared of snow, with the hummingbirds flitting above her as always, that the elephant started behaving rather strangely. He began flapping his ears and then lifted himself up on to his back legs briefly and then down again.

"What is it, Fingers?" asked Mimi, hurrying back over to him.

He tilted his massive elephant head to one side, as though listening, so Mimi did the same. She could just make out the faintest sound of a dog barking in the distance. Nothing more.

But Mimi knew from experience that not only was Fingers good at hearing sounds she herself often couldn't hear, but also that he was very good at pinpointing where they were coming from.

Fingers stared deep into Mimi's eyes. She made a decision, knocking on the door.

The little man opened it and could immediately see from the girl's expression that something was wrong.

"What is it?" he said.

"Will you look after Clip and Clop for me,

please?" she asked. "Old Mr Grunt can look after himself. He's used to it."

"Of course," said Jeremy. "Why the change of plan?"

"Fingers has obviously heard something that bothers him and what would bother him most would be Sunny in trouble."

"Then go!" said Jeremy with some urgency.

Mimi nodded at Fingers and moments later he was lifting her up in his trunk and placing her carefully on his back. All the while, Frizzle and Twist circled her head. She held on tight and they were off.

Fingers could move at a fair pace through the snow, but his movements were somewhat jerky, which made for a bumpy ride for Mimi. At one stage, when they were crossing a lane between fields, Fingers came to a sudden halt and felt around in the snow with the tip of his trunk. He pulled something out and passed it over his head to Mimi.

It was a string bag with some very familiar contents: Chocolate Biscuit, Sharpie, some frozen underwear (as stiff as boards) and some frozen-solid melons.

Mimi's heart sank. "Mrs Grunt would never abandon her cat doorstop unless she was in real trouble, Fingers … but at least it means we're on the right trail. Good work, Fingers!"

Now Fingers started off again and soon they were charging in the direction of Th rn ry rph n g f r B ys.

Sorry. That should, of course, be: The Ornery Orphanage for Boys.

Speedy McGinty pulled the flying goggles over her eyes, pressed the big green START button in front of her and her gyrocopter lurched

forward along the short runway, which had been of cleared of snow, behind her bungalow. This tiny aircraft – whose moving parts she'd sprayed with de-icer – looked little more than another of her aluminium wheelchairs with a rudder behind and rotor blades above, and a collapsible wheelchair strapped, folded, to the back. She looked like she was flying a helicopter chair. In next to no time she was airborne but where to search? She decided

following the course of the railway line was
as good an idea as any, if that was where the
Grunts were supposed to have come from.
But she soon changed her plans.

Why?

Because after about thirty minutes she
flew over a girl riding an elephant. She had
absolutely no doubt that the elephant was
Fingers, not just because she didn't think
there were many other elephants about but

because the elephant was being ridden by a girl who, even from this height, looked very pink AND had a couple of humming birds ducking and diving in circles above her head.

Speedy swooped in lower to take a closer look. She tried to keep enough distance so as not spook Fingers but get close enough for Mimi to recognise her.

Mimi looked across at the extraordinary little aircraft travelling just above her, over to her right. She recognised Speedy at once and pointed ahead as if to say that the others must be somewhere *thataway* (because that was where Fingers was leading her).

Speedy did a thumbs-up, then pulled the gyrocopter back above the treeline and flew ahead to keep an eye out for any sign of Sunny and the Grunts.

Sergeant Tooley was driving the police car down an iron-hard off-road track. To say that it was a bumpy ride was a bit of an understatement. Inspector Brown's police radio crackled to life next to her.

"Yes?" said Bruiser Brown. "Any news?"

"They found Officer Gumby, Inspector."

"Found?"

"He fell in a ditch last night, hurt his ankle. Couldn't move."

"He spent the night out in this weather?" the police inspector gasped.

"Apparently he's a funny shade of blue but should be fine, sir. He says Mr Grunt has been seized by the escaped prisoners but that Mrs Grunt and the boy are holed up at the Ornery Orphanage for Boys."

"The Ornery Orphanage for Boys,"

Inspector Brown instructed Tooley.

The sergeant swung the car off the road and into a field. "I'll have us there in no time," she said.

From her seat in the gyrocopter, Speedy McGinty could see some buildings up ahead with a courtyard, in the middle of which was what appeared to be a huge painted statue of a man tangled up in something. She flew lower for a closer look …

… just as Sunny and Mrs Grunt emerged through a doorway.

Speedy McGinty was about to shout and wave in relief when she noticed that Sunny was tied to Mrs Grunt who was tied to a giant bird who'd just emerged into the daylight after them.

She would like to have retreated to make

plans but the one thing the gyrocopter wasn't, despite its small size, was *quiet*. It sounded like an angry wasp trapped in a jam jar multiplied many, many, MANY times.

Rodders Lasenby had now come out into the courtyard too, and pointed up at Speedy. There was no love lost between those two.

They had a shared past. She made a quick decision, then swooped in dangerously low.

"Bees!" shouted Mrs Grunt. "Giant bees!"

Turning too sharply, the bottom of Speedy's gyrocopter just clipped the side of the statue. There was a splintering of stone and Albert Ornery's sandy-coloured moustache broke away and fell …

… fell

… fell

… directly on to the head of the false-facial-hair-loving Michael Jinx. It knocked him out cold before he could even let out a whine.

"Run!" shouted Sunny in the confusion that followed. He managed to break free from Twinkle – forcing Twinkle to let go of the makeshift rope he'd made from some of the orphans' dressing-gown cords – and dash towards an archway in the wall. Mrs

Grunt, who was attached to Sunny by the dressing-gown-cord rope, stumbled after him. They found themselves in the company of a delighted Mimi and Fingers. Mrs Grunt was even more delighted to see Mimi was clutching her string bag containing Chocolate Biscuit and Sharpie.

Speedy made sure she added to the confusion by sweeping and ducking and diving her machine.

Rodders Lasenby had had enough. He'd had enough of Michael Jinx's whining. He'd had enough of feeling threatened by Twinkle and his toothy dog. He'd had enough of Lord Bigg being even posher than he was and insisting on being called *Lord*. He'd even found Mandy mumbling through bandages was getting on his nerves. And the arrival of Speedy McGinty in one of her flying machines was the last straw.

So Rodders Lasenby made a run for it. He laughed to himself as he stumbled out across the courtyard, through the doorway in the wall and into the open countryside. He ran through the snow, his face broadening into a smile. This was real freedom, not having to spend another minute with those good for nothing—

He gasped. He felt the coils of a python wrap round his waist and squeeze him tight.

"I say! What the— Wait! No!"

He was being lifted off the ground.

"Help! Wh—"

This was no python. This was an elephant's trunk. This was Fingers and that wretched pink girl.

"Put me down this instant!" he yelled when realisation dawned.

Fingers turned him upside down and peered at him with one of his enormous eyes.

At the arrival of

Rodders Lasenby, the hummingbirds Frizzle and Twist took flight, abandoning their post

above Mimi's head. This had happened before. There was something about the man that these two birds really did *not* like.

Twinkle was the last man standing and was being severely bothered by the crazy woman in her little buzzy aircraft-thingy. He decided the best thing to do was to throw something at her. Throw something fast enough and heavy enough and he might knock her clean out of the sky with a direct hit.

He looked around for something to throw. The stone moustache had broken off quite cleanly, in a good boomerang shape. He could give that a go. He felt the weight of it in his hands – it was heavy – and gauged his throw, waiting for Speedy to bring the gyrocopter in low again.

Ready.

Take aim.

At that moment a frozen melon thrown by Sunny (taken from his mother's string bag) hit Twinkle in the stomach like a cannonball. Twinkle made the loudest "OOOPH!" humanly possible and doubled over in pain on top of the already unconscious Michael Jinx.

"Good shot, Sunny!" said Mrs Grunt, who was still attached to him. She was hugging Chocolate Biscuit and sitting on Rodders Lasenby, who was face-down in the snow.

But to their horror, Twinkle wasn't down for long. Roaring with rage, he struggled to his feet, his bird costume torn and one of the wings hanging free of his arm as though it were broken. Frizzle and Twist circled his head, pecking at his giant "beak". Twinkle tried swatting them away with his hands.

Fingers lolloped forward but there was

no way the elephant could fit through the doorway in the wall through which Sunny had so successfully lobbed the frozen melon.

Suddenly there was a loud CLANG and Twinkle toppled forward on to the cobbles. Miss Edna Ornery had hit him over the head with that most impressive frying pan of hers. She looked down at her victim and on her thin lips was a satisfied smile.

Chapter Thirteen

Round-Up

When Inspector Brown arrived on the scene he was greeted by Miss Ornery, frying pan in hand, and three of the escaped prisoners tied with dressing-gown cords to a large statue of her grandfather. Mrs Grunt was dancing around them.

He soon had them in his custody, safely locked up in the back of a police van. In next to no time, they'd be back in jail where they belonged. Twinkle had misjudged Miss Ornery. He hadn't tied her tight enough to

the kitchen chair and she and her frying pan had had *their* revenge.

Sunny, meanwhile, had gone off on the back of Fingers with Mimi, in search of Mr Grunt and his captors. Elephants have an amazingly sensitive sense of smell, and after raising his trunk and sniffing the wind a few times, Fingers lumbered off through the snow in the direction of the tractor barn.

Lord Bigg heard them coming and peered out through a gap in the planks. He knew the game was up. He and Mandy might have Mr Grunt, but they had an elephant and he'd heard police sirens in the distance.

"I'm leaving," he informed Mandy. "We tried. We failed. You do what you like. I'm off. Come with me if you like, or stay. Shark will probably hold them off for a while but the dog can't guard Mr Grunt and defend you at the same time."

When, with Sunny and Mimi on his back, Fingers reached the barn, Sunny called out, "Dad? Are you in there? Are you OK?"

A woman Sunny had never seen before stepped into the open doorway where the tractor had broken through the doors only the day before. She had Monty the parrot on her shoulder.

"Your father's fine," she said. "And I have Lord Bigg in custody."

Sunny and Mimi slid down off the elephant.

"Who are you?" asked Mimi.

"I'm Officer Mandy Cooling of the APB," said the woman, stepping aside to let them pass. Inside the barn they found Lord Bigg tied to a post with bandages that had only a matter of minutes before been hiding the woman's true identity.

Mr Grunt was sitting on – rather than in – his sack, playing with Shark. "You took your time, didn't you?" he asked Sunny. "I'm hungry." His face broke into a big grin.

"I love you too, Dad," said Sunny, giving him a big hug. "Mum's fine."

"What's the APB?" asked Mimi.

"The Animal Protection Bureau," said Officer Cooling. "I'm on the trail of a very rare bird's egg, stolen by Thomas 'Twinkle' Winkle."

"But how did dressing up as a mummy help?" asked Sunny, now patting Shark.

"Michael Jinx's sister, Mandy, was in a serious accident and I took her place," she said, cutting a long story short.

When the APB learned that Jinx had escaped from prison they'd suspected that he would want to visit his sister. Because she'd be unrecognisable, covered in bandages, they thought it a great opportunity to switch the real Mandy Jinx for an APB officer and Mandy Cooling was the one nearest her size and with similarly coloured eyes. The fact that her first name was Mandy too had nothing to do with it!

Lord Bigg struggled and tried to say something, but his bandage gag prevented him from speaking.

"So Mandy Cooling took the place of Mandy Jinx. But what was the point?" asked Mimi.

"Because you thought Michael Jinx and Twinkle might stick together and Twinkle might lead you to the missing egg!" said Sunny.

"Absolutely right!" said Mandy Cooling. "The first priority of the police was to capture the escapees. The first priority of the APB is to find and protect the egg."

"Then why didn't you go with Twinkle earlier?" said Mr Grunt. "Why stay with me and Lord Bigg?" Mr Grunt said the word "Bigg" as though it were the last type of cowpat you'd ever want to step in, accidentally or on purpose.

"Because I wanted to make sure you were unharmed," said Mandy Cooling. "Things had got out of hand."

"So Mr Gumby – and whoever he was minding that helium balloon for – are APB officers too?" asked Sunny.

"Yes," said Officer Cooling. "The balloon is used for observing the local area around Twinkle's house and aviary—"

"Aviary?"

"His garden is like one big netted cage," Mandy Cooling explained.

"I think we actually passed over that yesterday evening before we crashed!" said Sunny.

"More than likely," said Mandy. "Planes and helicopters are noisy and often give their presence away or arouse suspicion," she went on. "But no one thinks twice about a balloon except to think, *Isn't it pretty?*"

"You were watching Mrs Winkle to see if she'd lead you to the place where she's looking after the stolen egg while her husband was in jail?" asked Mimi. She was frowning because, as well as having Monty on her shoulder, Mandy Cooling now had Frizzle and Twist circling above her head.

"Yup, somewhere hot enough to keep the baby chick inside the egg warm enough to live and grow. But she rarely leaves the house."

The sound of Speedy's gyrocopter had been getting louder and louder and now she came in to land. It was difficult for Speedy to use her wheelchair in deep snow, so the others went out to greet her.

She was relieved to find Mr Grunt unharmed.

"And this is the dog that was supposed to be guarding you like a prisoner?" she asked him, patting Shark on the back. He licked her hand.

"I have a way with animals," Mandy Cooling explained. "They all seem to behave so NICELY when I'm around."

Later that day, back at the Ornery Orphanage for Boys – safe in the knowledge that all the escaped prisoners were back where they belonged and that Shark and Monty were being cared for by the Animal Protection Bureau – there was a family gathering. The caravan was there with Clip and Clop, and with

Old Mr Grunt fast asleep inside, clutching Maisy and blissfully unaware what was going on around him.

"Now, perhaps you can finish your story, Miss Ornery," said Sunny, holding Fingers' trunk for comfort. They were in a ground-floor sitting room, and despite the cold they had a window open especially for the elephant to stick his trunk through. "Can you tell me who my birth parents are?"

Edna Ornery looked down at her hands in her lap.

"I'm afraid I don't know, Sunny," she said at last. "You were left on the orphanage steps as a newborn and we took you in."

"Oh," said Sunny. It took a moment for the news – or lack of it – to sink in.

He didn't quite know what to think. He'd always assumed that if he ever found out which washing line he'd been rescued from he would find out who his birth parents were.

"There was a note," said Miss Ornery. "I've kept it safe all these years." She went over to a desk and opened a small drawer, pulling out a small piece of paper. She gave it to Sunny.

On it were the words:

PLEASE LOOK AFTER MY BOY
HE WILL ALWAYS BE MY
SUNSHINE

Mr Grunt squeezed Sunny's shoulder. "Well, blow me down with a rusty hairdryer," he said. "You're our sunshine too. Your mum even named you Sunny. So that proves it."

It was Mrs Grunt's turn to give her boy a squeeze. Bunny, who'd been snuggled up in the many layers of her clothes, crawled down her arm, out of the end of her sleeve, hopped up on to Sunny's head and sat there.

A week later, as the snows were beginning to thaw, a postman delivered a letter addressed to:

Sunny Grunt
The Caravan
Bigg Manor

Sunny was sitting on the steps of the caravan when the postman handed it to him. There was the official APB logo stamped on the back of the envelope.

"What's that?" asked Mimi.

"It's from Mandy Cooling," said Sunny. "I suggested where she might find the missing egg."

"You did?"

"I did. I didn't want to say anything to you, in case I was wrong. But I was right!"

Mimi snatched the letter from Sunny's hands and read it. "Clever clogs!" she laughed.

Sunny had remembered that when he'd flown over what he'd later discovered was Twinkle's aviary in the balloon, there was one square patch where the snow hadn't settled. It had reminded him of the roof of Lady "La-La" Bigg's pigsty whenever she gave Poppet one of his steaming-hot baths: the snow on the roof melted because of the heat. What if that square patch of the floor of the aviary was also a warm patch *that melted the snow*? What if it was warm because it was the roof of a building containing a toasty-warm incubator containing a rare, stolen egg? The police and the APB had searched the house and aviary a number of times but what, Sunny had suggested, if it was the roof of a secret *underground* room?

And, as Mandy Cooling's letter informed him, he'd been right. No wonder Mrs Winnie Winkle so rarely went out. The APB finally uncovered a hidden entrance in the kitchen broom cupboard leading to an old bunker under the back garden. There she lovingly cared for her husband's pride and joy: the stolen egg.

Included with the letter was a photo of a very young, very featherless bird of prey. It looked incredibly ugly yet somehow incredibly cute at the same time.

On the back was written:

Egg flown back home, returned to nest and reunited with parents. Successfully hatched.

Reunited with parents, thought Sunny.

He knew now he'd never meet his birth

290

parents. He looked at Mimi with Frizzle and Twist buzzing around her head as always, then beyond her to Fingers, who was busy patting Lady "La-La" Bigg's pig, Poppet, with his trunk. Clip and Clop looked on with a distinct lack of interest, chewing away at their breakfast.

Sunny had left Mr and Mrs Grunt upstairs in the caravan. They were still asleep in bed. Mr Grunt had his feet up by the headboard and his head down by the footboard. When he woke up he was going to be in a terrible muddle. Mrs Grunt, meanwhile, had carefully placed Sharpie on the floor where Mr Grunt was most likely to tread on him if he got up without looking. She was hugging Chocolate Biscuit and snoring a series of teeth-rattling snores.

Sunny smiled to himself and looked up at the bright morning sky.

Who needed birth parents when you had the Grunts?

TH ND

*Read more of the Grunts'
ridiculous antics in:*

THE GRUNTS IN TROUBLE
THE GRUNTS ALL AT SEA
THE GRUNTS IN A JAM

Search for

nosy crow

on the iTunes App Store for
the free Grunts game for your
iPhone, iPod Touch or iPad,
The Grunts: Beard of Bees

Check out the buzz at
www.meetthegrunts.com